WESTWARD

The Journey of Adolf Nagel

by

Harry Simpson

In Loving Memory

Of

Harry Herman Simpson, Sr.
October 14, 1882 to January 18, 1968

And

Elizabeth Jane (Oliver) Simpson
January 19, 1883 to September 8, 1980

DEDICATION

The conception of this book is based on the concept of FAMILY. It is the first in a series of books for the Nagel family. Specifically for me, this pertains to my family.

First is to my immediate family that provided me the love and caring to first experience life and to develop imagination.

- My father and mother – Harry Herman Simpson Jr. and Melva L. (Howard) Simpson.
- My five siblings – Anita L. Baugh, Rebecca A. Scott, John Laurence Simpson, Kirby L. Mongeau, and Lori Holmes

Second is to my family that allowed me to experience life through the eyes of adulthood caring for others.

- Sharyl Silvia (Langenbach, Alley) Simpson
- Jeffery D. Alley and Michael W. Alley

Third is to my extended family of relatives for that relationship provides perspective and the protective feeling of belonging.

PROLOGUE

Ever westward! That was the goal of those colonizing the New World. These brave travelers followed an internal instinct no different than what drove migrating birds in the fall and spring. For many, it was the dream to own their own land. To others, it was just curiosity about the unknown. To Adolf Nagel and his faithful friend, Oskar McGill, the westward journey was driven by the need to escape. Survival required fleeing a necessary killing and the resulting fallout of hatred and revenge.

Two seventeen year old young men left their hometown for a fresh start and, unbeknownst to them, they started a legacy. Driven to escape, they began a journey that took them to Missouri then onward to the Kansas Territory.

The simplicity of youthful action was coupled with the American concept of constant advancement. The new pioneers only meant to get away, become established, and bring Adolf's sweet Caroline to join them. Little did they know the impact they and their progeny would have on the infant United States.

Chapter 1

"Leave me alone!"

Caroline's voice startled Adolf as he tied Buck, his gray dun gelding trotter, to the top rail of the corral. He clutched a freshly picked batch of wildflowers in his left hand to win Caroline's smile. Unexpectedly, her voice had come from the barn, not the house.

He sprinted towards the open barn door, hastened on by the more panicked screams.

"Help! Let me go."

His piercing gray eyes quickly scanned the small barn. There was movement at the back. Caroline's arms were pinned to her sides by the forceful embrace of a man. The front of her dress was ripped to her waist and the unidentified man's face was pressed against her naked breasts.

Exploding with anger, Adolf flew forward, grabbed the man by the hair with his right hand, and ripped the man's head backward. The man's sound of protest was driven back into his mouth, as Adolf slammed his left fist into the man's face, smashing flowers as well as lips. He felt one tooth break off in a knuckle. Adolf's right fist was left holding nothing but a large amount of greasy blond hair as the man flew away. Continuing after him, Adolf drove his right elbow into an exposed nose that was crushed on impact, spraying blood everywhere. Hovering over the man, Adolf kicked him in the side and was pleased to hear the sound of broken ribs.

Adolf would have stomped on the man, but he felt Caroline's hand on his shoulder.

"Let him go. Help me to the house."

With one last look at the crumpled man, he turned and took Caroline into his arms. He helped her cover herself with the torn dress then guided her towards the sunlight.

"He's got a gun," gasped Caroline.

Her cry over-scored a slurred, "You're dead."

Shoving Caroline into the stall on the right, Adolf dropped to his right knee and instinctively tugged his pistol out of its holster as he spun around. An enormous gun blast preceded the whizzing bee sound of a lead ball piercing the space he had just vacated. He fired his Colt Paterson from his hip and was rewarded by an explosion of blood flying from both front and back of the man. A lead ball from Adolf's .36 Colt had plowed through the man's body.

The shocked face of the dead man was that of Nathan Coulter, the son of the wealthy owner of the town bank - Caldwell Coulter. Adolf didn't like either father or son. Both were rather pompous. He recalled that Nathan had attempted, to no avail, to court Caroline last month. But an attempt of rape? He could not get his mind around that.

Forgetting the puzzle, he focused on helping Caroline inside. Adolph asked gently, "Is your mom or dad home?" Mr. Adams had a gunsmith shop in the new settlement of Jackson in Hocking County, Ohio. Adolf liked him and his wife. They always treated him nice, even if they snickered about the 17 year old romancing their 16 year old daughter.

"Both are in the house. I wanted to give them space so I came to the barn to comb Betsy," Caroline trembled. Betsy was Caroline's black Tennessee Walker mare. "Nat jumped out of hiding and grabbed me." With that she burst into loud sobbing and her whole body began to tremble. "Thank you Adolf. I couldn't fight him off."

Adolf swept her into his arms and hurried to the house. His powerful six foot, 190 pound body easily handled the five foot, hundred pound beauty. Hard corded arms were the result of years of training horses – Trotters. His piercing gray eyes were even more intense than usual as he slammed open the front door and yelled for Caroline's parents. The door bounced off the front wall with a riveting bang that echoed through the immaculate house, bringing her parents on the run.

Paul Adams was trying to refasten the buttons of his shirt as he yelled, "What the hell is the racket?"

"What's wrong?" Mrs. Adams asked softly. She looked at them with her face turning white, "Is she hurt?" Although a little plump, Caroline's mom was still a very attractive lady in her fifties.

Adolf placed Caroline down on the couch and ensured her torn dress covered her breasts. He pulled the knitted quilt off the back of the couch and laid it on top of her.

Mrs. Adams crouched beside Caroline and tucked the quilt around her. Caroline was crying so hysterically she couldn't answer her parent's questions, so Adolf decided it was his to explain. Before he finished, an angry, red faced Mr. Adams grabbed the ten-gauge leaning by the front door and rushed outside.

A few minutes later he came back in still very angry and shouted, "That SOB's dead, alright. Thank you, Adolf."

Adolf stood back as the three Adams hugged each other. Frantically, Mr. Adams turned to Adolf, "You have got to get away from here. Caldwell is a powerful man. Sheriff Palmer is the brother of Caldwell's wife Hanna. That's how he got the job." Rubbing his chin, he looked at Caroline, "Adolf can't stay here. They'll sure hang him."

Caroline sobbed, "No. I love Adolf. He had to shoot Nathan. It was self-defense."

"If I run away they'll take it out on you all. I can't leave this on you." Adolf had a determined look on his young face.

"Caroline, tell him he has to go," Paul Adams said in a fatherly tone. "We will be all right. We will tell them the truth about Adolf shooting Nathan, but he must be gone or they will still surely stretch his neck."

Part of Adolf knew Mr. Adams was right, but he did not want to leave Caroline. Caroline placed both hands on his face, "When you get settled, come get me. I will always be yours."

With reluctance and after many kisses, Adolf rode to his dad's ranch where they raised and trained Trotters.[i]

His dad was in the barn getting acquainted with a six-week old strawberry roan. The smile ran off his face, like rain off a tin roof, when he saw his much troubled son. Adolf dismounted, tethered Buck to the apple tree, and shuffled toward the house. Olaf Nagel was a shorter, older version of his Adolf. They had the same lean hard body, brown hair, and hook nose, but Olaf's eyes were a gentle brown versus Adolf's piercing gray. Neither was handsome, but were both considered striking by the Hocking County women.

Olaf immediately guided the colt into the stall with her mother, and followed his son to the house. He found his wife Belinda already weeping against their son's broad chest. His questioning eyes searched his wife's face, pleading for an explanation.

Belinda ushered her two men to the kitchen table. She said, "I have fresh coffee, let me pour it. Then we can straighten it all out."

Adolf went through the whole event, including his killing of Nathan and the Adam's instructions to leave. His parents agreed that Adolf had to get out of the county. Adolf questioned them, "Where would I go?"

Mr. Nagel stated, "My brother Gottlieb's ranch in the Ozarks. Your uncle is breeding a new line of Trotters. He could use your help training them." He took his son's hand and continued, "You have to leave right now. Go! Take Buck."

Adolf was in the midst of packing Buck, a gray dun Trotter, when Oskar McGill exited the bunkhouse loaded down with his own gear.

"I'm goin' with you, and that's it."

Adolf didn't consider arguing. They had been best friends since first grade and both worked on the ranch. Unlike Adolf's preference for a clean-shaven face, Oskar always seemed to have two day's growth and a drooping red mustache that matched his bushy red hair.

Mrs. Nagel handed each boy a huge grain sack of food. "I made the biscuits this morning along with the bear claws, and I think the sausages and jerky should keep for a while."

Adolf's dad thrust his brand new .54 caliber Hawken rifle into Adolf's hands. "I was going to give this to you for Christmas." Mr. Nagel was the best shot in Hocking County. At the 4th of July rifle shoot he had won the rifle from the humbled Mr. Krueger. It was the only Hawken in the state.[ii]

Tears ran down from his eyes as Adolf took the offerings from the best parents in the world. He didn't want to leave them. They had taught him everything he knew and had showered him and his six brothers with love every day of their lives. "I always thought this is where I would stay all my life." His eyes wandered over the entire ranch lovingly, memorizing his familiar and comfortable home.

"You ready?" Oskar interrupted. He was doing his best to hold in his own tears. "Thank you Mr. and Mrs. Nagel for taking me in. Don't fret any. I'll take care of Adolf."

Mr. Nagel shook Adolf's hand with both of his own hands before stepping back for his wife to grab onto their son.

Belinda wept, "Oh Adolf. This is so hard. I thought I had you for a few more years. All my boys are out of the nest now."

Mr. Nagel peeled Belinda's arms from Adolf and whispered, "They gotta get."

Adolf mounted Buck and followed Oskar's paint gelding, Patches, toward the front gate. He took one last look at his parents to see them holding on to each other and waving.

"Bye," floated to him in his mom's tender voice, like the last leaf of autumn hitching a ride on a gentle breeze.

Chapter 2

Two more different young men could not be found. It was as obvious as a hairy wart on a pretty damsel's face. Both men were tall and hard, but their appearance clashed like wet and dry. It didn't take long to notice one was silent and one was not.

Adolf was just damn neat. His black calf-high black boots shined like sun rays bouncing off a polished tin cup. His pin striped two-tone gray trousers were carefully tucked into his boot tops. His cream and gray stripped shirt buttoned to the neck with a cream necktie carefully knotted. A formfitting charcoal gray vest, also with every button buttoned, was topped with an unbuttoned, hand-sewn brown leather waist jacket. The only crease in his tall, broad brimmed hat was the carefully placed dent at the very top center of the crown. He was the epitome of the strong silent type. His words were few but well thought out.

In contrast to Adolf, Oskar's bushy red hair completed the rest of his ruffled outer appearance. Flashing emerald green eyes were separated by a square nose with a chin-length droopy untrimmed mustache dangling beneath. Freckles, hundreds of rust freckles, exploded everywhere - face, arms, and hands. His appearance was almost sloppy. His rumpled cream-colored corduroy trousers appeared to have been balled up before they were pulled on. They were randomly stuck into scuffed cowboy boots. His wrinkly red plaid shirt was missing the top two buttons. Their absence was marked by hanging thread that gave space for a forest of red chest hair to burst outward in every direction. He wore a pass-me-down navy blue wool coat so dirty that it appeared to have spent most of its many years under his horse's hooves. The only item showing signs of care was the gray, short brimmed Derby tilted to one side.

Normally Adolf's silence was complemented by the out-of-control flow of nonsense sprouting from Oskar. Oskar was a habitual chatterbox, a magpie or a spooked killdeer drawing attention away from her nest.

Today there was only silence. Both young men were in deep thought. Part of Oskar's silence was out of respect for his best friend. A funeral parade could not have been more sober. Normally, both were in constant observation of their surroundings, but not today. Their heads faced straight ahead and their eyes were aimed inward, each to private thoughts.

Adolf was asking himself how things could get turned around so damn fast. A pleasant sunny day happily riding to visit his beloved reversed into the worst experience of his young life. What could he have done differently? These were the common questions following a catastrophe – the what if's.

Oskar's thoughts were more of the 'what' variety. What could he do to help Adolf? Normally Adolf was in control, but Oskar knew it was his duty today. His friend needed to be looked after and that was all there was to it. He also knew that his friend needed silence, not dumb banter.

Oskar became aware that the sun was about to set and it was up to him to find them a spot for the night. He cast his eyes around and saw an old barn ahead, the roof mostly still there. Without saying a word, he guided Patches towards the barn and Adolf instinctively followed.

Oskar dismounted and looked inside the barn for critters and to ensure the barn wasn't about to collapse before leading his horse in. Adolf's eyes followed Oskar like watching a rabbit cross his path. He also dismounted and led Buck into the barn. Each unsaddled his own horse, grained them from gunny sacks tied to the saddles, and used the saddle blankets to rub the horses down.

Oskar led the horses to a close-by creek and let them drink their fill before staking them to a patch of tall grass by the barn. Unlike himself, Adolf simply sat on his saddle and stared vacantly toward nothing. Oskar gathered sticks and some dry grass as kindling to build a fire just outside the barn door. He then cooked some beans and coffee. He took a plate of beans and a cup of coffee to Adolf.

After cleaning everything up, Oskar led the horses in and picketed them inside, as to not invite horse thieves. Without a word, the men settled into their beds and, fitfully, tried to sleep. Sometime before dawn, their tiredness took over and they slept to the peaceful sounds of their horses and the insects serenading each other.

Chapter 3

Using directions from one of his Uncle's letters, Adolf was setting a course south-west toward the North West corner of Kentucky. The natural, high speed walking pace of the two Trotters had brought them within a stone's throw of the state line in three days.

He appreciated the comfortable ride provided by the unique diagonal Trotter gait. Their right front and left rear, left front and right rear rhythm was very smooth for the rider – no bouncing, no bobbing. This ride provided a lot less wear-and-tear on the human body than all other horse breeds.

Although Adolf was still depressed, he was exhibiting it less. Looking at nature was like looking at a master's painting – it was the work of a master - God. Brilliant blue skies had accents of randomly placed clouds resembling cotton balls. Lower there was a multitude of greens – pine, spruce, balsam, juniper, maple, oak, elder and fruit trees. There were constant inserts of wild animals: mule deer, elk, an occasional bison or black bear, brown rabbits, gray and red squirrels, black and white skunks, roly-poly porcupines, and a multitude birds species.

Sight was not the only relaxing background sense– smell, hearing and even touch all joined hands to create an abundance of sensations. A continuous soothing message provided by the tender hands of God.

The peaceful background sounds of the various animals were joined in this musical of nature by the bubbling of a close-by creek, the hum of busy insects and, the constant nonsensical chatter of Oskar.

Nature's artist was signaling the approach of dusk by splashing the western sky with the brilliance of crimsons and oranges. Even various clouds were rushing to join in, hugging on the horizon to increase the brilliance of the sunset as the rays of the sun fought their way through.

A change in sound interrupted Adolf's dreamy state. Oskar's chipmunk-like chatter had stopped. A moment later, the higher pitched Oskar yelled, "Look over yonder. Ain't that a clearing?"

"Yes it is!" Adolf yelled back.

As they rode closer they could see a well-kept farm. Oskar pushed Patches close enough to almost rub Buck's shoulder so he could speak without yelling, "I declare! Ain't never seen nothing like that in my whole life. Now that's just darn neat."

"Suspect it to be Mormons," declared Adolf, "I heard tell their places are neat as all get out."

Oskar squeaked out, "Why there's nothing out of place, not even a fallen tree branch. Your dad keeps the ranch neat but that down there now that is super neat with a capital N."

Adolf ventured forth, "Let's ride down there. Mormons are supposed to be hospitable. They may let us sleep in the barn out of the elements."

"What elements? It's not going to rain and no wind is blowing. But I'd be just plum pleased if they'd invite us to supper," said Oskar hopefully.

They stopped their horses at the edge of the clearing within shouting distance of the spread. "Hey there house," hollered Adolf with his hand cupped around his mouth. His shout-out was rewarded with a bunch of movement – a gaggle of kids clamored from all over as if sprouting from nature. A woman in a long dress and funny bonnet came from the house carrying a shotgun as long as she was tall, and a man holding a pitchfork emerged from the barn.

Adolf hollered again, "We're friendly. May we approach?" He nodded to Oskar and they both raised their hands to show they were empty. The man said something to the woman and she pointed the shotgun to the ground but was ready to bring it into play if needed. The man yelled back, "Lower your hands and come on in, but keep them in sight and no sudden movement."

They noticed the tallest girl was holding a hog's leg that seemed to extend all the way to her knees. "Sure hope that flintlock ain't cocked," Oskar whispered as they lowered their hands and nudged their horses into the yard.

The farmers were Mormons and did invite them to supper. Adolf and Oskar were even invited to stay in the barn for the night. There were seven kids from the tall girl of about fifteen down to a diapered boy of less than one. After a rather long prayer, they dug into a table full of grub that could have fed an army troop. There were three or four types of meat, smashed potatoes, heaping bowls of vegetables, plates of steaming fresh bread, butter, several pitchers of milk and a whole lot of fresh-from-the-oven fruit pies.

Pleased with the spread, Oskar spoke up, "Why now, thank you for sharing a meal with us. That is very Christian like. I've never seen so much food all at the same meal." The woman lowered her head but not before they could see a pleased smile touch her mouth. The man didn't acknowledge the compliment, just started heaping food on his plate and passing things around.

With both elbows flying sideways, Oskar started right in shoveling food into his mouth. Adolf approached his food in the same manner that he wore his clothes - neat. All the kids kept sneaking peaks at the two men and then giggling. Adolf felt he should check if he had something on his face, but reckoned it was just normal kid behavior around strangers.

The tallest girl was pushing food around her plate with her head lowered, while sliding peak-a-boo looks at Oskar with flirty cyes. Damned if Oskar wasn't sneaking peaks back. Twice Adolf kicked Oskar under the table. This was a religious family and the girl was clearly only fifteen or so, but the way she kept her shoulders back to emphasize her full woman's chest got across the message that she felt she was a full grown woman that could get a man's attention. Damn if she didn't have Oskar's. He was only seventeen himself.

The older girls helped their mom clean up the dishes while Peter Gaillard invited the two well-fed visitors to join him to smoke a pipe. Neither smoked, but did join him to converse about the farm and get information of the land ahead. The family had relatives in Kentucky, so the talk was informative.

During the smoke, Mr. Gaillard told the boys they could spread their bed rolls in the barn without even being asked. Downright hospitable. The two boys checked on their horses and then placed their bed rolls on top of straw spread in an empty stall next to Buck and Patches. As they were preparing for bed, Adolf asked in an annoyed voice, "Damn it Oskar. What you doing flirting with that girl? We're guests and they're Mormons."

"You mean Sarah? Why she started it and she's right like pretty," Oskar defended.

"Keep your damn sausage in you trousers or you're going to get us shot. Get some sleep and quit your smiling."

Chapter 4

Adolf knew he had not slept long when a change in the night sounds shook him awake, just as if his mom had jostled his shoulder. Isolating each sound in turn, he detected: random horse movements, creaks of the barn walls, insects calling to each other, and the night breeze tickling leaves on the trees. He recognized no change. He peeked over to Oskar. Ozkar was rubbing his eyes. Something had woken him also.

Then there was a whisper, "Psst, psst, hey you awake?" Someone was tip-toeing into their sleeping area.

Oskar's whisper echoed back, "Yah. That you, Sarah?"

There was a flirty response, "Yes. Wanna go to the loft with me?"

Ozkar replied quietly with a lecherous, "Damn right." Then there was a swishing of Oskar's bare feet sliding through the straw. A quick peek verified he was only in his underwear. A female giggle was joined by a male exclamation, "Damn, you're naked!" The giggles were then replaced by heavy breathing and a lot of rustling of straw. There was a louder, "My God, you're randy," then straw rained through the ceiling cracks like a summer cloud burst. Attempts to be quiet were soon forgotten as passion became the prime focus. Male grunts playing base to soprano moans and other whispered female encouragements.

Even Adolf's hands over his ears could not keep out the groans or the kettle-drum like pounding against the boards overhead. No matter how hard he tried, memories of his thirteenth-year introduction to sex trampled through his head, like a cattle stampede - visions of luscious Sally Cramer.

It began as a tranquil fishing escape one Sunday afternoon. But it was interrupted by a very soft, "Hi." Walking from behind the elderberry bushes was sexy Sally – the first girl in his 8th grade class to develop full sized tits. Well, those two points of interest were thrust forward against a thin blue blouse; a tantalizing pose that made him forget fishing. His blood made a rapid rush heading below his belt when she coyly asked, "You want to trade peeks?'

"Peeks of what?" he stammered not daring to believe she meant what his mind was flashing.

She ducked her head and slyly slid out the words, "You know what." Hell, not only unexpected but damn mind blowing. Adolf had to pinch himself to see if he was having a daydream.

The best line he could think of was a sophisticated, "Suuurrre."

Sally planted a damn wet kiss on Adolf's mouth and started pulling her clothes off. He froze and stared, before remembering he was to undress too. He yanked his clothes off without taking his eyes from the most amazing sight he had ever seen – a naked woman, not a girl, a woman. The thatch of hair below was the same blond as on her head. Her breasts were the size of honeydews, but softer and with pick nubs sticking out from lighter pink circles. He was confused as to where to focus his attention.

"You want to touch them? Cause I sure want to touch that," she pointed at his fully extended witching rod, throbbing with each heartbeat. It seemed more excited than Adolf. It was so full of blood it hurt.

It didn't take long for her to convince him they needed to do more than look and touch. After squirting all over her thighs on his first try, the two bounced all over that hidden grove several times before laying exhausted side by side listening to the deep voices of bull frogs shouting their approval. Breeze blown leafs overhead seemed to be adding their enthusiastic applause.

Adolf's memories were interrupted when Oskar tapped him on the arm and said, "Sarah wants to know if you want a turn."

"Tell her no thanks. I'm going to stay true to Caroline."

"Fine with me. I'm going to go again," smiled Oskar as he clamored back to the loft. Damn, Adolf didn't want to see his bare butt, disgusting.

Adolf must have fallen asleep and the two lovers must have had enough because a rooster was crowing and sunrays were marching in the door like spilled water running downhill.

Back at the house, the young men were saying their goodbyes. All mothers must read from the same book. Mrs. Gaillard handed both of the boys large chicken feed gunny sacks as she said, "There's fresh bread and beef sandwiches along with some homemade sugar coated donuts."

Mr. Gaillard shook hands with them, "You young fellas take care and know we will pray to our Lord to watch over you." Adolf appreciated his words, but could not keep from being shocked by the brazenness of Sarah throwing kisses at Oskar over her parents' shoulders. Being naive just did not include stupidly putting his friend's nuts at risk. There was no damn excuse for Oskar compounding the risk with the lustful, cow looks Oskar was openly displaying back. Adolf nudged Buck a couple steps to hide Oskar and hoped he would restrain himself. Adolf was thinking they had to get going before they got horse whipped, shot, hanged, or maybe all three.

Adolf nudged Buck into Patches to force them onto the trail. His uneasiness raised prickles on the back of his neck. Ant-like sensations crawled up and down his spine until they were well out of rifle range. Then Adolf could no longer keep his anger roped up tightly. He screamed at his friend, "Have you no damn common sense?" They had been best friends since they both cast off diapers and attached their wagons to take on the world together. But gosh darn it, there was no excuse for throwing caution to the wind and putting both their skinny necks into hemp nooses.

Adolf wanted to read to Oskar from the Book –'The wild dove had given him all he was ever going to get from her. Cast it to the winds and pull the damn horns in.' Instead he said, "Your damn foolishness is going to make this one short ride. I don't want all we're ever going to be shit piled by your brainless dick muddling in some one-time soaking."

The blush that galloped across Ozkar's face like a runaway prairie fire indicated he was a sorry soul, even though he painted a round-mouthed expression of confusion to his face. Adolf knew nothing else he said would tighten Oskar's run-a-way free nature so he clammed up and silently stalked ole Buck towards Missouri and the wild out yonder.

Chapter 5

Ever since he was too big to straddle and ride pigs, Adolf had worked from rubbing sleep from his eyes to too dark to see. His felt his dad's disapproving eyes and shaking head stretching across the traveled miles. Taking his time like this was just plain wasteful, but the sights were even better than watching a frisky new colt taking a trial run on brand-new, shaky legs.

A rotation of Indian braves from various tribes sprouted periodically on the horizon to observe Oskar and Adolf. They recognized some tribes, but most they did not. The Shawnee of Ohio were plentiful, then they recognized Kickapoo, Miami, and even Potawatomi but other groups of watchers they had never seen before.[iii]

Two groups of Indians had even charged them as if to count coup, but had stopped short when the boys stood behind trees with their long rifle barrels extended. After chanting and waving weapons, both Indian groups had turned and ridden off.

One afternoon, small birds sprang from the left side grove of trees like a huge puff of smoke. They circled and chose the trees on the right to land. "See that?" whispered Oskar.

"Yah. Something or somebody," Adolf whispered back. "Distract them for me if somebody's foul intentions present a situation." He eased the eleven inch Colt Paterson out and held it down his right leg. He advanced the cylinder away from the empty chamber and cocked the hammer

"Good spot to rein in gents." A voice loudly filled their ears as a raggedly dressed, scruffy whiskered codger stepped from behind the trunk of a dead oak. He held a Kentucky long rifle pointed at Adolf. The rifle had seen its last cleaning about a century ago. After spitting out a glob of tobacco juice, it mostly flowing down his chin to merge with its cousins on the front of a once yellow shirt, the disgusting man showed brown teeth and suggested, "Get on off dem rides and show me all yah got to gift me."

Adolf held his saddle horn with his left hand and swung his left leg over his saddle. His Colt Paterson was still hidden by his right leg.

Oskar stuck both hands into the high blue and went into his best scared pilgrim imitation. "Please don't shoot. I'm only seventeen and still a virgin. Never seen the elephant nor touched any titties. You can have my twenty dollar gold piece, just spare my life. Please mister." It almost drew Adolf's attention.

All this shrill jabbering turned the would-be highwayman's eyes to stare in shock at this horseback spectacle. Damned if his gun didn't follow like it was attached to his eyes with some invisible string. At the very last moment, he noticed Adolf's hog leg rested on Buck's saddle. It was aimed dead toward him. The highwayman tried to swing his awkward long rifle back to Adolf, but by then Adolf's ball was already in midair. It tapped on his filthy shirt before blowing through his rigid body. Red blood, black smoke, and an ear splitting boom joined the world. In response birds flew out of every tree in the grove and the dumb gent's corpse dropped like a bag of old clothes.

"Now, he was sure obliging," Adolf grinned. He carefully nudged the mess on the ground with his boot toe ,while insuring his shine didn't get ruined. He turned to Oskar and said, "You might want to go on stage. If that was an act it sure was believable."

They decided the long gun was not worth keeping so they left it and the body where they lay and rode off without appearing to give a second thought to the temporary interruption.

Although Adolf acted nonchalantly, having now killed two men did bother him. He was brought up in a Christian home and was taught from the Bible. He was sure the killings were necessary, but they still played on his mind. It also made him ask himself if he was doing the right thing by running away. He missed Caroline and his parents a lot. He had always just accepted his life would be in Ohio forever. Caroline and he had talked about getting married and settling on his parents' ranch until they could afford to buy their own place and raise a batch of little Nagels. It was his parents that suggested going to Missouri, but was he a coward for doing it or was he letting his parents get him out of trouble like a mindless kid? Should he have stayed and faced it head on? He sure didn't want to leave that life. What if Caroline fell in love with someone else? He didn't even have any idea how he was going to bring her to where he would be. Gad, it could be years before they would get together again.

He interrupted Oskar's usual chatter to ask, "Are we doing the right thing here by going all that way to Missouri?" Adolf reined Buck to a stop and faced his friend.

Oskar brought Patches to a stop and frowned at his friend, trying to get an idea of the direction the conversation had gone. "What you talking about?"

"I was wondering if I am a coward for running away from Ohio." Adolf looked at his friend and continued, "It all happened so damn fast and we were on the road before I could wrap my mind around the whole mess."

"Damn, you sure do think too much." Oskar shook his head, "There was no other choice. Those stinking Caldwell's are worthless bastards, but they are rich and powerful. They and their kin, the sheriff, would have hung you with no trial. Yah got that?"

Adolf looked hard at Oskar before breaking into a big grin. "I knew there was some reason I liked you for a friend, but never thought you would teach me common sense." He chuckled, "Thanks Oskar. You're right and you helped get my head on straight, but don't expect a thank you kiss."

Oskar chuckled back, "So I did learn you something. Heh, heh." Then he smiled and said, "Always wandered if you were partial to boys. Never thought you wanted to kiss me though. Now I'll have to sleep with one eye open."

Oskar kept busting into laughter for the next several days. Each time he wondered to himself, "How about that? Old smarty pants listened to dumb ole me."

Adolf had to work hard to not laugh himself, but he sure couldn't do that or his friend would have to put out money for a larger hat to fit his swollen head. But, then again, he was glad his friend had said what he did. Adolf still didn't like running away but he accepted it was the right thing to do.

Chapter 6

A couple days later they were looking down into the famous metropolis of St. Louis. "Look at that there," Oskar said with much awe, "Never seen so many people pinched together in all my day. How do they know which breath is theirs to use?"

As normal, Adolf didn't utter a sound. He used his heels to send Buck into St. Louis and its 14,000 mixed variety of people. With a continual string of nonsense, Oskar followed .

Stepping their horses through the scatter of pedestrians, horses, and wagons, they advanced down the wide busy street. Other streets meandered to other areas, but this seemed to be the one with all the various business establishments – and what a variety they were. Some were even recognizable. There were several liveries, eating places, and general stores, but outnumbering the rest where the saloons. They came in all forms, from tents to two story buildings with batwing doors. Standing on the balconies of the two-story saloons were scantily dressed women yelling 'how-di-dos' to every man that passed by.

Adolf was pretending to stare straight ahead, but Oskar was almost twisting his darn head off gawking like a kid at a circus. He even took his hat off and yelled 'howdy' to all the painted doves. But it didn't seem like anyone noticed, so Adolf put his embarrassment back in his pocket.

Their attention was drawn to a circle of men raising dust in front of a red front saloon. It was tagged as the *Bull Horn* by hand-painted, two-foot tall letters on a six foot plank nailed above the batwings. The young men stopped their horses to watch the spectacle. Eight men of various ages, sizes, and dress were ringed around the largest man they had ever seen.

He was well over their six feet and huge like from a fairy tale. Broad shoulders and ham-like upper arms leading to plate-sized hands were contrasted by a belly the size of a beer keg. The belly spoke of fat that didn't exist. This slab-like body was all hard, with well-developed layers of muscle on top of more muscle. He would have seemed like a monster but for the clean homespun shirt and overalls that yelled 'farmer' and the innocent, reddened face topped with yellow hair that dangled in front of his eyes. His smashed hat was upside down on the roadway as testament to the violence being directed toward him.

His robin egg blue eyes were darting around the circle, trying to determine who was going to attack him. One of the men threw a rusty horseshoe that bounced off the back of the giant's head, bringing a spurt of blood before escaping to the roadway. With a bellow the huge man reached down to grasp the horseshoe with both hands. His face became even redder as his cheeks puffed out and his back muscles strained. Slowly the horseshoe changed shape until it was straight and then became a twisted imitation of a pretzel.

The crowd that had formed yelled out surprised bursts of awe and there was even some clapping at the circus strongman-like display of strength. The ring of men only hesitated a moment, but regained courage by their number advantage and renewed their efforts to torment the stranger.

Oskar knew that Adolf was a stalwart champion of fair-play so he was ready to follow suit when he heard Adolf's, "Get away from him." No one paid Adolf any mind until he fired Mr. Paterson into the sky and yelled, "I said leave him alone, you damn cowards!"

Without knowing the issue or any of the men, Adolf had chosen sides to even the odds. He knew Oskar would follow right along.

"None of your damn business," stated the oldest of the mob.

Adolf didn't have to say anything because his eyes spoke for him. None of the eight men could look long into Adolf's angry eyes without feeling an unexplained shiver of apprehension bring self-survival to their sobering thoughts. Because Adolf's gaze, and gun, seemed to be focused on the speaker, he was the first to grumble and walk away. The others watched him, glanced at each other for courage, and, seeing none, eased away one by one.

Without anything to watch the rest of the crowd also dispersed. The only remaining person was the giant blond farmer. He picked up his hat and tried to pound it back into its original shape. Holding the still misshapen hat in hand, he walked over to the horsemen. "Thanks. I was in a real pickle as to how I was going to escape getting a life threatening beating."

With a childlike smile, the obvious Scandinavian stuck his huge paw out and said, "I'm Sven, Sven Nelson from up Minnesota way."

Adolf and Oskar holstered their Colt Paterson's and leaned down with their smaller paws extended to become swallowed up by the largest hand either had ever seen.

"Can I buy you a beer?", Sven offered.

Adolf and Oskar dismounted and threw clove hitches on the closest rail. "Sounds dang friendly to me," Oskar replied and followed Sven into the *Bull's Horn*. Without a word, Adolf trailed behind all the way to a homebuilt polished pine bar.

It was early afternoon, but the room seemed to be half full already. "Lots of slackers in this world," thought Adolf.

A chubby man with a bald-head and a face full of brown whiskers said, "What can I get you gents?"

Sven spoke out, "Three mugs for my new friends and me. You betcha." These last words were a give-away of his Swedish heredity.

Oskar chanted, "Here, here," and reached for the first mug that was slid onto the bar top. The next two beers were claimed by Adolf and Sven.

Blowing the two inch foam off his beer, Sven raised his mug towards the two traveling young men. "Thank you again. And may this be the beginning of a longtime friendship." He then clanged his mug against the other two mugs with such gusto that it was a surprise to all in the room that the mugs remained intact.

Sven was interested in Oskar's story of the men's travels. Once he had been brought up to date, he started his own tale as to his reason for leaving Minnesota. He had just got into his story of the Nelsons and eight other families leaving Sweden to settle in Taylor Falls, Minnesota when they were rudely interrupted. Most of the original mob had reunited along with a couple of new, alcohol encouraged ruffians.

"Yah ain't got no gun in my face now pilgrim. Man enough to face me alone?" The antagonizing voice came from one of the original group. He was addressing Adolf with his hands tightened into fists. His face was red from anger or alcohol, maybe both.

Adolf didn't even turn around to acknowledge the alcohol induced bully. He sipped his beer and stared straight ahead.

Oskar, knowing his quiet friend, did likewise, Sven looked at both with an unspoken question and decided to try following the example of his new friends. He restarted describing the new homestead in Minnesota.

"Hey Fancy Dan, I'm challenging you." The self-appointed mob leader had bragged to his buddies and was sure he could whip this fancy dressed skunk. "Turn around girly. Unlessens you're damn yellow?"

Adolf didn't even flinch, he just stared straight ahead. Now the bully was sure he had a coward to contend with. "You going to cry for your bitch mommy and pee your pantaloons."

"Oops," thought Oskar. The ignorant pissant had stepped across the line. Did he really refer to Adolf's sweet mom as a bitch?

Adolf still stared straight ahead and brought his beer up for a sip. The over-confident, puffed-up toad jostled Adolf's arm, spilling a slosh of beer. The beer didn't get a chance to reach the floor before the mug smashed into the would-be bully's face. Blood jumped as the mug shattered and sliced into his face. Before the bully could even yell, Adolf turned and drove his right knee into a wide-open space well known for carrying the family jewels. Bending forward, the bully expelled a bucket of whatever was rotting in his stomach. Adolf drove his fist down on the back of the exposed neck. The unconscious man's face splashed into the vomit on the floor.

"Bar man, would you get my friend a new beer?" Oskar addressed the open-mouthed bartender. His was the only sound in the tomb-like bar.

"What the hell?" The biggest bully of the remaining mob exclaimed. He stepped towards Adolf, "I am going to break every bone in your sissy body." The man was just over six foot and had his sleeves rolled to his elbows, displaying huge forearms. The scars on his face suggested he liked to fight, and he smelled like he was a teamster, which he was.

He swung a fist that never reached its destination. A loud smack was heard. Sven's plate-sized hand stopped the fist in midair. The surprised man started groaning as the sound of crunching bones echoed loudly throughout the bar. You just can't fix stupid, so the dummy threw a second punch, which Sven caught with his other hand. He then twisted both of the man's arms downward. The man pranced up onto his tip toes. A couple of loud pops joined the snapping of bones as both arms separated from their shoulder sockets. Thankfully, he passed out and Sven let him fall onto his buddy.

The next sound was that of boots hitting the floor as the mob's remnants rushed through the batwings.

"Damn," Oskar said, "There's none left for me." He started giggling as he slapped Sven on the back and said, "Now, please continue your story. I was finding it damn interesting."

Adolf didn't even acknowledge that anything had happened. He simply sipped his new beer and opened his ears to take in his new friend's history.

Chapter 7

Having no determined destination, Sven accepted their offer to travel with them to Missouri. They had seen enough of St. Louis and were on the last leg of the trip. Apprehension of the unknown was being crowded out by excitement of the new. Sven exhibited a huge giant-sized smile as he fell in behind Oskar and settled into an Adolf-like silence. Now both Sven and Adolf half listened to Oskar's ceaseless babble. Not only was he content, for the first time in his life, Sven felt he really belonged.

Three days later, they stepped into the only saloon in some three-hole town in southern Missouri to get directions to the ranch. They knew they were within striking distance and were anxious to learn the last piece of the puzzle.

Saloon was a little bit of a stretch for what they walked into. It was half a dugout and the rest an old military tent. It stunk of mildew, unwashed bodies, and beer. The word 'Saloon' was hand-painted in barn red on the tent next to the opening. There was a wooden four step drop to the dirt floor. The bar top was a roughhewn plank eight foot by eighteen inches by four inches. A few polished wear spots on the bar top mingled with a week's worth of spilled beer. Splinters were dangerously sprouting everywhere.

The rest of the saloon consisted of a couple of old tables, a few mismatched chairs, and four thrown together plank benches. Although early in the day, the bar was mostly full. There were all old codgers of every size and shape, wearing every description in the English language for clothes. The filthiest man Adolf had ever seen was smashing flies against the bar top with his bare hand. He was very short and skinny. There were about six strands of gray hair combed atop his pink head as his only virtue of hygiene. His longish nose was bright red with a roadmap of blue veins. He used the back of one hand to wipe his leaking nose. His once white, now gray shirt was missing three buttons and was covered with a vest that must have been found somewhere in a dump.

Understandably, no one else was at the disgusting bar. The trio of young men went there anyway. They very gingerly stood close to the bar, making sure not to touch it. They noticed dead flies across the bar, along with a gallon jar containing what looked like boiled eggs in swamp water. All three immediately lost their appetites.

The one consistency in the bar was that the all these ancient customers were sporting guns, of every vintage and shape imaginable. One even had an old blunderbuss lying on the table alongside a half-full glass of something.

The smoke filled room had got real quiet. The old gents were staring with open mouths at the trio of young men. They had to admit no three men less resembled each other and it was pretty obvious that they were not regulars.

"Only got beer and it's warm," the bartender interrupted the silence. If they had known where else to obtain directions, they would have walked back out. Instead, they ordered three beers, and soon regretted it. The chipped mugs were so dirty you couldn't tell the color of the beer.

Adolf dropped fifteen cents onto the bar and turned around without touching his beer. "Anyone know where the Slash N ranch is?"

Sound started back up as if this needed heavy discussion by the aged customers.

A skinny creature with white whiskers stood up and walked towards them carrying something that resembled a beer mug. "Ya know Gottlieb, do ya?" The old man smiled to display a mouth with about two yellow teeth. "I was their cook sometime back in the ages. Mr. Nagel is the fairest dang boss man in the country."

He got real friendly when Adolf told him Gottlieb was his uncle. "You tell Mr. Nagel that ole Charlie Stroble says howdy do."

Happy to help relatives of Gottlieb, the old man told them how to find the ranch. They bought the old timer a beer, but didn't touch theirs as they left the bar and mounted their horses. Sven's horse was a grullo (blue dun) quarter horse stallion, which he called Blue. It stood seventeen hands tall with sturdy hind quarters, but still Sven made it look like a pony.

"Did yah ever see so much filth?" asked Oskar as they trotted out of the spot in the road. "I may never drink another beer. My ole tummy is still afraid I was going to put some of that filth in it. It is still yelling 'no' at me."

Sven spoke up, "Ain't Saturday, but I feel like bathing right now. That was the grossest place I ever did see. It makes a smelly hog sty seem down tight clean."

Adolf didn't say anything, but a shiver ran up and down his body. He rubbed his hands on his pants legs just in case he had touched something in the saloon.

After a few miles, they all got quiet, deep in thought of what the end of their journey would bring. Even Oskar was silent as they rode the final leg into a new life.

Chapter 8

There it was! Surrounded by rolling hills of beautiful wooded land sat a sprawling log cabin, two large barns of roughhewn planks, a long log bunkhouse, a cook shed and several other outbuildings. Scattered throughout was a checkerboard of corrals constructed of two-rail fences that hemmed in Trotters. Four magnificent breeding stallions each stood in their own corral. The other four corrals contained brood mares and their foals. Over a thousand acres of open field displayed about three hundred grazing mares and colts of a vast number of colors.

Three well-fed mutts barked their announcement of strangers, and then ambled toward the horsemen with tails wagging like flags in a parade. A large man in his fifties stood in the door opening of the barn, shielding his eyes with his hand. He reached back into the barn to produce what looked to be a hand-held cannon, but Adolf knew was a very long ten gauge double barrel. A couple of boys Adolf's age moved out of the second barn with rifles cradled casually in their arms. Another teenager followed them with a short scatter gun pointed down and long shiny black hair catching sail in the breeze. Adolf took a second look at this teenager as his brain registered he was looking at a raven haired, beautiful young woman.

The screen door screeched open to another woman. She also had black hair, but with streaks of silver twinkling in the rays of sun. Adolf stopped Buck, raised his hands and hollered, "Hey the house." From the corner of his eyes he saw Oskar and Sven also raise their hands. Adolf silently prayed Oskar was keeping his eyes under control. He sure didn't want to get shot by relatives.

"I'm family," Adolf yelled, "I'm Olaf's son, Adolf."

A moment of stillness, then whooping and hollering climbed up the hill like a raging river over a dam. Uncle Gottlieb lowered his shotgun and yelled, "Ride on in nephew! You're plenty welcome. Ma, you believe this? Boil some coffee. Hey gang, let's welcome your ornery cousin and his pards."

By the time the visitors reached the house all five relatives were standing by the front door. Adolf's uncle reached Buck in three long strides and gripped his nephew's hand with both of his. He was pumping away like he expected water to gush forth. "We are mighty pleased to see you. Wow, you're all growed up."

Stepping back he commanded, "Come down off that horse and give your Aunt Ailish a big howdy-do hug."

After proper introductions, Adolf's cousins, Bill and Henry, grabbed the horse reins. Henry announced, "We'll take them to the barns and rub them down."

For the next hour or so, all eight were filling the kitchen plumb full of excited hob-knobbing. Empty pie plates stacked all over the oak table amongst full cups of steaming coffee. Seemed to Adolf like the cups were self-filling. Between Aunt Ailish and cousin Neale (the sixteen year old raven haired beauty) the coffee kept on coming.

That night Adolf and his traveling partners were situated in the bunk house. His aunt argued that Adolf should stay in the house, but Uncle Gottlieb understood and persuaded her otherwise.

The three had the bunkhouse to themselves seeing as the three hired ranch hands were out looking for signs of horse thieves. A couple of horses were missing. No carcasses were found and Uncle Gottlieb knew the horses sure hadn't taken off for greener pastures by themselves. He suspected horse thieves of the two legged category.

Although both Oscar and Sven were star struck by Adolf's cousin Neale, they had kept from embarrassing him. The relatives were impressed by the horse knowledge of all three so Uncle Gottlieb offered them all jobs on the ranch. That sure done pleased Adolf. He had been afraid they might have to split up. Hiring three hands all at once would seem weird for most, but Oskar and Adolf knew that training Trotters was labor intensive. Handling foals began very early. Halters were put on at eight weeks so the colts could begin learning to be led. Usually by the tenth week of their young life, daily handling had begun so they would become comfortable and trusting with humans.

Adolf listened to the excited chatter of his friends and was proud that they didn't exchange any risqué thoughts of cousin Neale. Both seemed to know that kind of talk was way off limit.

The young men were so tuckered out from the ride and the excitement of meeting Adolf's extended family that it didn't take long to start sawing wood, each engrossed in their own private dreams of their new future.

Chapter 9

A few weeks had gone by and the three were blending into the Slash N routine. Uncle Gottlieb was tickled pink with both Oskar's and Adolf's knowledge and skill for training Trotters. But he seemed even more taken with Sven's blacksmith and horse doctoring talents. Well now, everyone on the ranch seemed to find chores around Sven when his oversized hammer reverberated against iron in the smithing shed.

The other three hired hands had come in and they turned out to be easy to take a liking to. The oldest was a grizzled fifty-eight year old codger with the handle of Shorty Sweatzbar, obviously German. He said he had answered to Shorty so long that even he didn't remember his given name. Like his name, he only stood about five foot five inches with his boots on.

Then there were the young 'uns as Shorty called them – Milton Reimer, a Mormon, and Timothy O'Conner. Timothy, he did not like to go by Tim, was Ailish's Irish nephew. Both young men were in their late thirties, which didn't seem young to Adolf and his friends, but it depended on your perspective.

Bill and Henry spent most their free time at the bunkhouse with the hired help. The backgrounds of all eight were so diverse that it made for some damn interesting conversations, but eventually the talk always came back to the missing horses. Another three horses had disappeared. Loyalty of hired help to the brand was well known and was no exception here. Stealing from their boss was no different than stealing from them themselves and not tolerated.

Shorty rubbed his whiskered chin and grumbled, "I don't like this none. Reminds me of some past experience." He took the time to pinch a batch of chaw to pack behind his upper lip. He seemed to gaze far away into the past. "Them other times proved to be hombres checking out how easy it was going to be. They then walked off with most of the string ever durn time."

The bunk house got very quiet as everybody contemplated this unwelcomed revelation.

It was Sven who first broke the silence, "We are not going to let that happen to the Slash N. We got to put an end to this now."

Oskar spoke up, "Any Injuns been raiding?"

Bill answered, "Not stealing stuff. The Kanzas[iv] tribe is notorious for stealing horses but they have never ventured this far south. They raid up north in the central Kansas territory."

Henry asked, "Any ideas? Dad told Bill and me to ask if anybody had some ideas to stop this before we lose more horses."

Sven announced, "You betcha. I learned to track pretty darn good while hunting deer and such in the Minnesota forests. I spent some time with a couple tame Sioux north of our homestead. Learned a hat full, you betcha." He continued, "If your pappy don't give a mind, I would like to ride Adolf and Oskar out yonder and see what we can find."

"Sounds like a plan. I'll ask dad tonight," Henry nodded his head as he responded.

Bill's head was also nodding as he echoed his brother, "I like it. Sven, can you really track?"

Oskar and Adolf lowered their heads, but a smile blossomed on Sven's face. Proudly he stated. "You betcha I can. To hunt in them full grown white pines and hemlocks, you learn or go hungry."

The next morning Mr. Nagel stood beside the three young men as they tied behind their saddles the gunny sacks his wife had loaded with food enough for three days. "I sure appreciate this, but you guys make darn sure to be careful, hear? Those horses are not worth tossing away your future. You got slickers? Rain sneaks up sudden like in these here hills."

Adolf hid a grin. It reminded him of his own dad playing mother hen. His uncle was more nervous than a wet behind the ears boy getting his first peek under the skirts.

All three had taken their guns apart and oiled them before reloading. They filled their belt loops, ammunition pouches, and pockets with ammunition and slung full powder horns across over their shoulders. Before leaving St. Louis, they had talked Sven into replacing his single shot pistol with a five shot revolver Colt Paterson like theirs, so they sure enough had firepower.

Adolf put his hand on his uncle's shoulder and, with a broad smile, stated, "Don't fret. We'll be all right."

His uncle placed his hand on top of Adolf's and squeezed. He then stepped back and waved his arm with a round-about motion like he was drawing a hole in the morning air. "Get on out of here."

The three musketeer replicas mounted and clicked at their steeds to march forward, with Sven astride Blue in the lead.

Chapter 10

The weather was not uncomfortable, but there was decidedly a chill in
the air. The deciduous trees were still clothed in their alternating shades
of green, but the chill reminded Adolf that a blanket of snow and nut-
freezing cold was in the near future. That cold and snow would not start
today.

Never-ending rolling green hills sandwiched the lush meadow grasses,
both providing contrasting shades of green. Scattered about as if
randomly tossed by a farmer drunk on homemade corn liquor were
various species of wild flowers – yellow bladder pod and evening
primrose, blue mist flowers, violet Johnny-jump-up, and white
arrowhead. Contently grazing horses were slowly meandering, choosing
their favorite flavors. If Adolf ignored that they were hunting for horse
thieves, the ride could easily be a daydream.

As they approached the flowing herd of mares and colts, Sven advised
the others on what to look for: indentations, bent grass, browning leaves
dangling from snapped branches, and tufts of horse hair snagged on
branches or even tall weeds. All of this was common sense, but a new
set of knowledge for Adolf and Oskar.

"Let's circle the pasture out a ways from the herd's graze." Sven
directed, "Adolf on the south side, Oskar here, and I'll mosey out
yonder. Shout a holler if your eyes light on something."

Good plan, thought Adolf as he galloped Buck to the other side of the
meadow. He dismounted and, holding Buck's reins, he scanned the

ground. He sneaked a peek at his friends and chuckled out loud. Oskar was also dismounted, but Sven had Blue in a steady trot and was leaning from the saddle to complete his search. Pretty plain who was the experienced tracker.

His feet were not bashful about reminding him that his tall-heeled boots were for riding, not walking. After a couple hours, Adolf forgot about his feet complaining when he recognized Oskar's excited, "Yahoo! Look at that."

Adolf turned towards Sven to see his reaction, only to notice Sven was about a quarter mile due west of the herd, deeply engrossed in following something. Oskar's second shout-out penetrated through Sven's concentration and his head snapped around. Cantering toward Oskar, Sven motioned for Adolf to follow

The blades of grass bent northwards, dried leaves dangling from broken tiny branches, and rocks with scratch marks stood out like gathering storm clouds. "Someone came in from this animal trail," mumbled Sven. "Over west is another trail of five horses leaving the pasture. Let's see where this one leads first."

The narrow trail dictated a single file formation. Yee gads, Oskar was so full of pride that it was a surprise his hat still fit and didn't scrape on the sides of the game trail.

The trail zigzagged, indicating the trailblazing animals' instincts to follow the path of least resistance. Adolf surmised the trail was used often by larger game such as elk, maybe even bear, which made it large enough for horses. His mind visited a multitude of possibilities for what the trail might have in store for them. There could be an angry ma bear protecting young'uns. Or what if it was far wandering Kanzas after all? They sure couldn't escape backward on this winding trail. Was that their destiny – scalps on the spear of some savages?

Sven tuned in his saddle and put a finger to his lips in the universal sign of 'keep you damn mouths shut.' He had stopped Blue and was rubbing the horse's neck to keep him silent. He dismounted, ground-reined Blue, and tip toed back.

After dismounting, Oskar and Adolf huddled with Sven. "There's a clearing ahead. Stay here, I'm going to take a look-see," Sven instructed. Then Sven walked up the trail and returned only a few minutes later. "You won't believe this, but there's about thirty or more horses ahead. Looks like a camp on the far side. What you want to do Adolf?" It was obvious that the leadership role was changing since the tracking was done. Adolf was the unannounced leader of the group and was expected to tell them their next step.

"Let's tie our horses here. Sure don't want them trading talk with the rest of them horses and warning them horse thieves," ordered Adolf, taking the leadership in stride. They checked their matching Colt Paterson revolvers to make sure the cylinders were not clogged with some trail pick up and loaded the fifth chamber, which they kept empty under the hammer when not in use. They had talked Sven into buying one in St. Louis for $35. Adolf and Oskar had bought theirs from Mt. Adams for his cost of $20.[v]

They slid the Patersons in and out of their holsters to insure they would not get caught if a fast draw was needed, but didn't put the tie strap in place. Adolf advised, "Leave the long guns. Don't know how many we're going find and single shots will be cumbersome." He did tug out his long ten gauge shot gun and check the loads. This gun was devastating at close range and it sure did make anyone on the business end think twice.

At the clearing, Adolf crouched down to be below the backs of the horses. Sven and Oskar did the same as they edged towards the small herd. They all froze in spot when several of the Trotters, for they were all Trotters, raised their heads and ears. A couple of whinnies warned that the herd was aware of them. After a while it was apparent that either no one was here or they were not paying any attention to the horse's announcements.

Patting several horses to quiet them down as they walked by, they were able to reach the far side. A nicker here and there seemed to be a sign from the horses that the three young men were not considered predators, so all the horses returned to pulling upper lips back to munch on the favorable meadow plants.

About sixty yards from the herd were hastily thrown together lean-tos. Grouped around a camp fire were seven scrubby looking men of all sizes in various costumes – from trapper-like buckskin to rumpled suits more appropriate for town clerks than for on the range.

The tantalizing smells of coffee and grease cooked deer meat, beans, and bread wafted across the fall breeze to remind the trio that it was nigh on lunch time and their stomachs were on schedule. It was also obvious that this group of desperadoes were way too confident. No one was guarding the camp. Additionally, they did not have the more modern guns that the three young men had. Each had several guns but all of the single shot variety. The number advantage was overturned by superior gun power.

No one wanted to risk getting shot, but the stealing had to come to an end. Sven moved about 15 yards left while Oskar did the same to the right, leaving Adolf and the large pattern spray of the ten gauge in the center.

They crept to about twenty yards from the men and Adolf yelled out, "Don't move. First movement is going to cause all hell to come down." Heads swung around and hands moved towards weapons, but then the world froze in time. At first there was shock, then fear, but they reverted back to the overconfidence of numbers. None seemed to notice the magnitude of firepower aimed at them.

The whispering of some dummy giving commands seemed to have their attention and they all slowly shifted their bodies as preparation to take the offense. Stupid! All of them. Just plain stupid.

"Now!" was shouted from the midst of the gang and they moved like puppets connected to the same string.

As if attached to that string, the blast of the shotgun and two Paterson's sounded as one enormous eruption. The shotgun blast of both barrels was like a scythe through barley as it plowed into the center of the moving outlaws. Then Adolf's revolver joined the other two colts until the seven bandits were nothing but a pile of red-splotched, torn rags wrapped around deflated life forms.

The only sounds remaining were those of horses vacating the vicinity and a few moans of dying men, contemplating their mistake while gasping their last breaths. Then even those sounds drifted away as a deathly silence settled upon the camp.

None of the three friends had received a scratch, primarily because their opponents had fired very few shots. After checking for survivors, none were found, the solemn young men squatted to the ground without saying a word.

Adolf was holding tears in. He knew tears were the natural letting go of tension, but he also knew his mind was at battle. Brought up under the Golden Rule, he hated violence but knew everybody had to wade through crap every day. His dad had talked to him about stuff like this and told him that you just had to pull your big boy pants up and move on.

A sob escaped from Oskar. Adolf glanced at his friend who had his face scrunched tight like a bitch dog expelling new pups and knew he was trying not to open the floodgates, but failing. Tears were running down bloodless cheeks like a spring river topping the dam. Sounding like the neglected hinges of a screen door, Oskar squeaked, "Why, damn it. Why? Were they plain too dumb? They made us kill them all dead."

No one had an answer for the pain of each of their internal struggles. Sven was looking at his boot tops, but actually seeing a replay of the mayhem. Then, without warning, a sour smelling stream flew from his mouth to cover his boots with steamy yellow stomach bile.

Adolf jumped to his feet and ran behind the first lean-to to heave his own guts as did Oskar. Then without another word all three moved to round up the horses that the outlaws had tied to nearby saplings and saddled them. Adolf mounted one and rode to retrieve their own horses, while Oskar and Sven gathered anything worth salvaging – weapons, gun belts, and pocket money. This was all bundled in a blanket and tied to the back of one of the outlaws' horses.

Their Christian upbringings said bury the corpses, but having no shovels justified the acceptance of leaving them for the scavengers.

They herded up the Trotters and followed the other trail toward where Sven had seen it. "I make out a Circle P brand on most of them horses, long with a few Triple D's, and seven Slash N's. Uncle Gottlieb will know who the other brands belong to," after these directions, Adolf quieted. Before long, Oskar's normal babble was accompanying the small herd and riders.

Back at the Slash N, the three musketeers were greeted to a hero's welcome – back-slapping, pumping of hands, and even hugging from Adolf's aunt and cousin. Adolf noticed his friends seemed to hold Neale's hug extra-long. Thank God for Oskar's desire to flap his gums. He enthusiastically described the happenings over and over with Sven filling in the detail. Adolf sat back and felt a sense of accomplishment along with pride for his two sidekicks.

Chapter 11

Activity at the Slash N reverted to normal, or what is normal for raising Trotters. Unlike ranches relying on bronco busting, the training of Trotters requires familiarizing each foal to human contact through hands-on patting of the nose and ears and rubbing of the legs. Obtaining their trust is essential, so frequent and kind treatment is used to dissipate fear and let them know they are not going to be hurt. The training progresses using a process that begins at six weeks of age. They first become familiar with the halter, then they are attached to a lead rope following their mother, finally they are on their own being led by a loose rein.

By 18 months they are ready to start getting used to a bit in their mouth, and able to be fit for their first set of shoes. This training is followed by getting them used to the saddle. They next are mounted, but not yet ridden. Acceptance of the human is natural and their first ride is not fearful to them. The final step is teaching the three gaits; which require teamwork with one person on the horse and one on the ground.

Sven was not familiar with Trotter training, but his blacksmith skills fit right in. The training was done by all except Sven and Ailish. The hiring of Oskar and Adolf freed Gottlieb to supervise and attend to record keeping. Keeping accurate records for each horse is important because each mare must pass through a certain number of cycles between each breeding. Records are also required to produce the desired line of Trotters, or for the ranchers in the Ozarks to produce the new Trotter breed – Missouri Fox Trotters. Aunt Ailish took care of the cooking since there were only eleven mouths to feed. In addition to doing her fair share of the training, Neale helped her mom clean up after supper.

Winter pushed Fall aside, snow fell, and the temperature dropped. The colts and their mothers were restricted to the barns. The first huge barn was for the colts under 18 months and Uncle Gottlieb had designed and built one that fit the training. Along each wall were stalls for the mares with their young. Each had an inside gate opening to the center aisle and an individual door taking them to their outdoor communal pens. These were kept closed for the worst part of winter. The back third of the barn was one large area for training, except for a storage room for grain and a tack room. A loft extended the entire barn with trap doors to drop hay into feeding troughs.

The second large barn contained individual stalls for the colts over 18 months. Also housed in that barn was the library where the records were kept, along with a desk for Uncle Gottlieb.

The training of the colts had cousin Neale hanging out with the guys. Adolf overheard Neale's one-time discussion with Oskar after a day filled with Oskar's attempt to flirt. Neale grabbed Oskar's arm at the end of the work day and led him to one of the unoccupied stalls. Oskar was grinning from ear to ear and Adolf knew he was thinking of special treatment, just not the same that Neale had in mind. Adolf slipped into the next stall to be close enough to waylay any shenanigans from randy ole Oskar.

Adolf was not ready for Neale's speech, "I like you Oskar, but as a friend only. These past days you have been underfoot every darn time I turned around. Dad is not going to allow you to be a slacker and I damn well ain't going to get all gooey eyed and let you into my private areas. Yah get it? No way, no day! You're cute alright, but I ain't interested, so tuck your horns in and be a friend or else."

Adolf sneaked right back out. Damn, his cousin sure didn't need his butting in. She was one tough cookie. Adolf did notice that Oskar and Neale seemed to become close buddies but Ozkar hung up his romancing spurs. Adolf didn't know if Oskar told Sven but Sven never misbehaved with Neale either. She had become just one of the gang.

After supper Bill, Neale, Oskar, Sven and Adolf would hang out together and trade insulting jabs or get into lengthy discussions. Adolf had become an avid reader during grade school and his two cousins were also. Although Oskar and Sven were less learned, they were no dummies, so they could hold their own. Of course Bill, Neale and Oskar were the more outspoken. Adolf and Sven listened mostly.

The days of constant work and the interesting evenings moved winter right along. Suddenly, snow was melting and the deciduous trees were sprouting green buds. Mamma nature had waived her good old wand and the cold took off in a huff. Coats were forgotten. Mr. Sun climbed higher in the sky and the birds chirped their thank you. Mud quit clinging to the boots and the windows got washed.

The stallions turned their calendars and demanded girlfriends. Selected mares were seeded and new foals were swelling up the mares' bellies. All the various tribes of insects filled the air, fleeing from birds' hungry due to building new homes.

Chapter 12

Sven was at his anvil taking a break to wipe well-earned sweat from his face and to appreciate all the sights; so, he was the first to notice a visitor struggling up the trail. The newcomer appeared to be hurt or darn played out, cause be was staggering and lurching all over creation. Sven yelled to the barn and scampered toward the man who had finally fallen on his face.

Adolf and Neale had almost caught up to Sven when he kneeled by the man on the ground. Whoever he was, he was covered in dirt, his shirt was torn and his hatless hair was messed up - looked like he had walked through a tornado.

As Sven turned him over on his back, Neale blurted out, "That's Mr. Schultz, Luther Schultz. He rides for the Triple D. It's about five miles south. Is he hurt?"

Adolf dropped to his knees and started examining Mr. Schultz. "Don't see any wounds or blood, but he looks like he has been to hell and back." Mr. Schultz's eyes were open but were fearfully rolling about without seeing.

"Injuns. Injuns got them all," were the first words out of his mouth when his wandering eyes started to focus.

Adolf shook him to bring him about, "What you mean? Injuns got who?"

Mr. Schultz rose up on his elbows and said, "Everybody on the *Triple D.* They're all dead and scalped." Then he panicked again and tried to jerk away, "They'll come here. Tell Mr. Nagel. We got to hide."

Neale said, "Take him to the house. Dad will know what to do."

Adolf stepped back as Sven picked the man up like he was no more than a toddler. They fast-walked to the house.

Mrs. Nagel ran a cool washcloth over Luther's face while waiting for Adolf to return with his uncle.

"Where is he?" shouted Mr. Nagel as he threw open the front door. Adolf was right behind him and they heard others running to the house.

"Mr. Nagel, I'm Luther Schultz from over at the Triple D. Redskins took the ranch." He paled as he continued, "Oh my God. Bodies every which way. Bloodied and hair lifted."

Gottlieb grabbed ahold of Luther's shirt and pulled him upwards. "What the hell are you saying?"

Luther focused on Mr. Nagel's red face and seemed to become aware of where he was. "I was at the outhouse and heard screaming and shooting from all over. I was scared and so I just peeked out." He started sobbing and continued, "It was over so damn fast." He started full-out crying like a young two-year old missing his mommy, "I'm sorry. Nothing I could do. Mr. Dvork was all shot up by the barn and they were lifting his hair. The Missus was under the clothes line with washing scattered all asunder. She was bloodied up and her hair was already gone. Walt and Bartholomew was done butchered by the tool shed and poor Charlie Druthers was screaming his head off as them Injuns were sticking arrows in him liken he was a pin cushion."

Adolf's aunt took Luther's head and hugged it to her bosom, "Shush now. You're safe with us."

Luther's eyes sprang open and he reached out for Adolf's uncle. "They'll be here shortly. They're after the horses. They got all ours."

Gottlieb turned to the front door as Henry and Shorty ran in. "Get everybody and have them saddle horses and grab their guns. We got to head the Indians off before they get to the house and horses."

Luther yelled, "Saddle me one and gimme a gun. I'm coming too.

Just like a field general, Gottlieb handed out the plan for battle, "Henry, take Shorty, Milton, and Sven with you. Sneak through those trees and get up the trail to the clearing. I'll take Bill, Adolf, Oskar, Timothy, and Luther and we will fort up amongst those rocks half way up. You let them pass and we will have them boxed in." He turned to his wife and daughter, "You two stay here and board up the house. If they get through, take the tunnel escape to the woods and hide." He ignored the frowns on the women's faces as he turned back to Henry, "When you hear our shooting set a trap for any escaping Indians, but be darn mindful that any left behind with the Triple D horses don't get you from your backside.

"Now everybody be careful. The horses don't mean diddly-squat compared to your lives. You all hear?" He ran over to his women folk and planted a kiss on each one. He held onto Ailish's hand one last moment and then declared, "Let's get this over with."

Henry and his band rode single file up a game trail, while Gottlieb's group dismounted at the rocks. "A couple of you tie the horses good back there off the trail," ordered Gottlieb.

The rocks looked like they had been hand placed for this very reason. Some were as large as a train car, but most were not. Most were the size of a large horse and they were stacked all over. Gottlieb stationed his men with some on top of the big boulders and all behind good shelter. They had a great view as the trail ran straight here for about 300 yards.

Adolf took out his Hawkens and several .54 cartridges and laid them in front of him. He also set the long 10 gauge to the left of the Hawkens after checking that both were loaded. He checked his Colt Paterson and tested to insure it would not get hung up in his holster. He remembered to take his hat off so it wouldn't tip the Indians off.

Waiting was the worst part and his nerves were starting to dance jig steps across his back. He looked over to Oskar on top of the neighboring boulder. He had prepared the same as Adolf, even remembered to set his hat aside. Adolf knew his friend was tense, even though he really didn't look it. Ozkar wore a shit-eating grin. Oskar glanced over to Adolf, and they each tipped a finger to their forehead and whispered, "Good shooting."

The world stood still in silence except for the casual whizzing of insects and chirping of contented birds. Periodically the rustlings of small creatures taking a hike in the trees floated up to their ears. Then a low rumble came in from the distance. Horses at a gallop were approaching. Then the sounds of horses were much closer and partially muffled by the soft trail grass. Indians were coming toward them.

Their peaceful view disappeared. Mounted Indians exploded around the bend of the trail. If they did not elicit instant fear, Adolf would have found them picturesque. Colorful clothed Osage astride decorated paint ponies were charging as a well-trained cavalry unit. The wearing of war paint and wide headbands with a single feather standing straight up in back verified they were of the southern Missouri Osage tribe and not the suspected far wandering Kanzas horse thieves.

Adolf felt his butthole pucker as old man panic tapped him on the shoulder. He had seen a few isolated Osage on the trip from St. Louis, but he sure didn't know much about them. Uncle Gottlieb's voice softly commanded, "Don't shoot until I do."

Adolf began to wonder if that had been his imagination because the charging horses seemed about to run them over, then a loud *BAM* caused the trees to throw out hundreds of birds, like leaves falling up instead of down.

Adolf felt the hammer-like recoil of the big Hawkens against his shoulder and the short Indian on the right threw his arms up as his chest turned red. Adolf pulled his Colt and executed five-well aimed shots. He knew all had hit various warriors. It looked like the Indians had hit an invisible wall as the hot lead kept slamming into them. The hillside was awash with blue smoke, but Adolf saw some of the Indians were still coming. He grabbed the long shotgun and lined it on the closest enemy. He pulled both hammers back, but triggered only the right side barrel. As the spreading shot disintegrated his target, he shifted his aim to the left and triggered again with a similar result.

Complete calm had engulfed his being. He calmly retrieved his revolver, punched out the smoking empties, and reloaded. Carefully looking down his barrel, he started picking off retreating Indians. Then it got real quiet as the few remaining attackers and many riderless horses rode around the far bend.

Seeing nothing left to shoot at, Adolf saved his last two shots and started punching out the three empties. Then a distant explosion of gunfire registered that Henry and his guys had sprung their trap. The initial explosion was follow by single shots of a battle clean-up variety. Only then did Adolf notice the broken arrows laying all-round him – some whole but most snapped from striking his boulder. The whole area was clouded in smoke, but it was starting to clear enough that the horrible mass of mangled Indians and horses were visible.

Adolf's body started to shake so badly that he couldn't grip his pistol. He leaned it on the rock, which was scarred up with fresh chips. Uncle Gottlieb hollered, "You all right? Any one hit?" That question was followed by sounds of movement as the men first checked themselves, than friendlies.

Starting to panic, Adolf looked to his left and yelled, "Oskar! You okay?" Hearing no response, Adolf quickly stood up and yelled again, "Oskar?"

Ozkar squeaked out a response, "I'm fine. Just an arrow burn on my shoulder. How about you?"

"Damn it! Next time answer faster. You caused me a fright."

Adolf heard his friend chuckle and say, "That mean you want to marry me?" Oskar burst out laughing, more as a release of fear than humor.

"Nah. Just feared I had to pen a letter to your ma and pa," joked Adolf weakly.

Chapter 13

Adolf and Ozkar grabbed their weapons and climbed down to check on the others. They were expecting to find excited comrades, but all cheer evaporated as they saw the slack jaw of Gottlieb. He looked up and said, "How're you two?"

Oskar told him they were okay. Adolf stayed silent, wondering what was wrong. They had won hadn't they? Adolf then noticed Luther and Bill were not standing with the others. "Luther bought the farm," Uncle Gottlieb said with tears streaking his cheeks. "Bill got an arrow sticking plumb through his thigh. Didn't hit no bone though, so he's okay to ride."

Timothy was wrapping strips of his shirt around Bill's his left leg. Bill was holding a blood covered souvenir.

"Adolf and Oskar come with me. We better check out that there pile. Be damn careful! Some Indians take a notion to play possum. Any question just shoot 'em and sort it out later," ordered Gottlieb.

The only shots they fired were to finish off some paining horses. There were seventeen forever silent Indians walking towards the happy hunting ground to join their dead ancestors.

Adolf and Oskar climbed on their horses and Adolf shouted, "We'll go check on the others." No shots were being fired, but they kept their revolvers in hand just in case. They rode up on another stack of dead Indians. The tangled mix of horse flesh and human was evidence that their enemy had been unsuspecting at this end too. Eight more Osage were trailing the other warriors to the happy hunting ground, but Milton Reimer, a Slash N wrangler, was no longer. An arrow was sticking through his neck and there were two more in his stomach.

Noticing the young men, Henry spoke up, "Your friend Sven is hurt real bad. One is in his hip and one in his chest. We left the one in his chest, because if it is in a lung, pulling it out could leak all his air."

Adolf and Oskar hustled to Sven. He was in pain and just barely awake. Shorty was taking care of him and looked up when the boys approached. The old codger had a face full of wet, "I'm right sorry, boys. He's a tough ole bird and I think he will fight off the grim reaper."

The Indians out on the meadow with the Triple D herd had taken off with the horses when they saw the main part of their war party was wiped out. Gottlieb figured the group would come back later to dig a hole for the dead Indians and horses.

They placed the bodies of Milton and Luther in the tack room to be prepared for burial. Of course Bill was carried to his room in the house, but Mrs. Nagel also demanded flat out that Sven be placed in a guest bedroom. They snipped the arrow head off and pulled the shaft back very carefully. The bleeding was steady and there was no sign of escaping air bubbles, so they were sure it didn't puncture the lung. Mrs. Nagel ran warm water through the puncture and then alcohol. She plugged both holes with boiled strips of cloth and tightly wrapped his chest. Because Naela was there, Sven tried extra hard to act as if it didn't hurt, but the beads of sweat on his ghost-white face said otherwise. He sure wasn't going to be running any races for a long while.

Aunt Ailish announced in a firm voice, "Neale, I'm going be busy with Bill, you look after Sven and the rest of you get outta here. He needs rest." Adolf and Oskar were twirling their hats in their hands with funeral-like faces as they stood beside the bed, until Ailish pushed her hands at them and said, "Shoo now. Let him rest."

After a slight hesitation both young friends shuffled out of the room. Adolf was relieved, but he noticed Oskar looked back and forth from Sven to Neale with what was truly a hint of jealousy.

Uncle Gottlieb had everybody gathered in the front yard. As soon as the two comrades stepped out, he ordered, "Timothy and Oskar hook up horses to the two wagons. Adolf and Shorty get all the shovels you can find. Henry, I remember some pulleys and tackle in the south shed. Throw what we got on the wagons."

Gottlieb's commands snapped everyone out of the glums and far away stares. Men hustled off with determination and relief for something to do. Out of respect for being the oldest, Shorty was assigned guard duty to watch for any Indians coming back. The rest of the men, including Gottlieb, piled corpses into the wagons and dragged horseflesh a ways out in the clearing for the scavengers to feast upon.

"We'll take all these bodies to the Triple D with them there. We'll take care of the dead Triple D folks and then dig a pit for these," Gottlieb directed.

Despite knowing what they were going to find at the Triple D, the men stood in shock as they looked at the horror displayed. A couple men stepped aside to puke and all had tears flowing freely and unashamedly. One by one, they went to work. First they dug individual graves side by side, then found blankets in the house to roll each Triple D resident in, and placed them in each grave. They placed Aaron and Hanna Dvork under a tall oak and Walt, Charlie and Bartholomew about fifteen feet away.

The men stood beside the graves and Uncle Gottlieb said the word of God for the deceased. The others stood in reverence, each with their own thoughts. After the graves were mounded, Gottlieb stated to no one in particular, "We'll make up some markers at the ranch and bring them back later. I'll write to their two boys in St. Louis."

That worked as the instruction to start the task of digging a big hole at the edge of the clearing. After the Indians were in the mass grave, Uncle Gottlieb said, "Go to the barn and see if they got any lime to cover the bodies."

It was past dark when the men and wagons returned to their ranch. No one seemed hungry and they were so tuckered that everyone crawled into their beds. Each man tried to set the horrible day out of his mind, and each man failed.

Chapter 14

After a couple weeks, the ranch had settled down and pushed the Indian skirmish into the past in order to concentrate on current events. Uncle Gottlieb and Henry had spread news of the Indian happenings to the neighboring ranches and settlers. Mr. Ambler, owner of the trading post fifteen miles east had to travel to St. Louis for a wagonload of shelf filler-uppers and volunteered to carry Gottlieb's post to the Dvork brothers. The brothers began their trip after receiving Gottlieb's letter. Otto and Benjamin had shown up yesterday with their wives and a whole wagonload of little Dvorks.

The screaming and hollering of young ones sticking their noses into everything on the ranch was replaced by a wonderful return to peacefulness when all the young Dvorks were herded back into the wagons to follow Gottlieb to the Triple D.

When Adolf's uncle returned, he grouped all the hands and told them the brothers were going to stay on and take over the ranch. Gottlieb said he was going to give them twenty mares to start up a new herd. "I'll let them use Big Charley for stud." Big Charley is a huge chested zebra dun, Morgan stallion.

In addition to Big Charlie, the Slash N had three other stallions: a handsome clay back, or Red Dun, Arabian named Sir Lancelot, a sleek black Tennessee Walker called Speedball, and a Palomino Missouri Fox Trotter[vi] tagged with the name Pale Beauty. The Slash N earned extra money by charging fees for stud services, because most of the nearby breeders did not have their own stallions.

Mr. Nagel told his hands that he had provided the mares in exchange for first choice of two foals each of the next ten years. He would charge the Triple D his standard stud fee rate. Henry spoke up, "That seems to be a pretty generous deal for the Dvorks."

Uncle Gottlieb chuckled and said, "Well it's fair to get them started back with a herd. But consider they pay for all the grain and the risk of what offspring is produced. Then we step in and get the best each year. I can live with that.

"Henry, pick fifteen of the Fox Trotter mares and five of the Saddlebreds. Check the records and insure you split the mares out over a three year span of those to be bred."

Uncle Gottlieb started to the house but stopped and yelled back, "Hey Shorty, know any good hands looking for a job? We will have to replace Milton and the Dvork brothers are going to need one or two themselves." Then he grinned at Shorty, "Not saying you spend a lot of time bending your elbow at the Antler bar, but maybe."

Shorty glared at Gottlieb then burst out with a roaring laugh, "You got me Mr. Nagel. I will listen up."

That Friday, Shorty returned from a night of testing the devil's brew. He brought home a tall skinny Texan. The bunk house was full of sawing logs, so no one knew until the next morning.

Adolf was the first to rouse and saw five beds had lumps instead of four. Had Sven been kicked out of the house? As he approached the bunk, he heard Oskar say, "Who's that?"

His voice woke Timothy, but not Shorty. The three men ringed the extra body and Oskar said out loud, "I sure don't know who the hell that is."

The stranger came awake in a hurry and rubbed his eyes with the back of a hand that looked like it had never met soap and water. He got a scared look when he saw three sets of eyes looking down at him. He let out a loud, "Hey Shorty. Where are you?"

Timothy kicked Shorty's bed and Shorty shot up clinging to his hog leg, "Who done that?"

The stranger's voice whined, "Shorty, who is these varmints?"

After all were up and no one got shot, Shorty explained that this 52 year-old cowboy was Eliza Swayne, or Slim. No one questioned the nickname. He looked like a walking chicken neck with whiskers. He was 5' 9", but only about 125 pounds with hat and boots on. Slim claimed he was from San Antonio and been a horse wrangler since there were horses.

The dirt covering him and the sour smell taking away every one's breathing air told them he was mighty past due for a bath. In spite of that inconvenience, he was plenty likable. They wished him well as Shorty took him to the house to plead with Adolf's uncle.

The crew was soaking up the last of the sausage gravy before he came back, which was a blessing because the yellow waves of putrid arrived minutes before he did. Oskar was the first to give up holding his breath as he blurted, "You ever taken a washing? You stink worse than a week old coyote carcass rotting in the sun."

Slim waved a hand at his arm pit and sniffed. "Am somewhat ripe, huh?" Then he proudly changed the topic, "I got the job, you all."

The banging of a screen door spun heads towards the house. Henry was striding over with a bar of lye soap in his hand. He stopped short of the table as if he ran into a stink wall. He underhanded the bar of lye towards Slim and pointed to the water tank. "Get or we will do it for you. I bet dad is passed out in the house. Mom is opening every dang window to air the house out. If you don't want to be shot for a skunk, you change your habits damn quick and, for god sake, burn those clothes."

Slim turned mighty red, and without taking time to breakfast, took off on a dead run. He stopped at the bunkhouse for clean clothes from his saddlebags and then to the water tank for a much needed dunking. Timothy grumbled, "The birds are even staying out of that toxic yeller air around him. Yee gods, I never."

Chapter 15

The next month was busy around the ranch, but every evening Oskar and
Adolf visited Sven and laughed like school kids. Neale joined in most
of the time. Sven was not bashful with her anymore. It seemed like the
four had been friends for many years rather than less than a year. If you
pretended she wasn't a beautiful girl, well she was even easy to talk
with. It even became normal to ignore that she sometimes placed her
hand on Sven's arm while chatting and Sven didn't even flinch.

Sven had taken to strolling around the ranch and even fingering the
blacksmith tools with a fondness as if hankering to start pounding again.
The men commented that Sven always had a shadow named Neale
walking with him. The shy Sven seemed to be quite talkative with his
new guardian.

Oskar and Adolf got to know the cleaned up Slim and spent many
evening hunkering down in conversation. All three had spent their lives
around horses, so they had a lot of common interests. But their
conversations seemed to drift to Slim's fawn colored mustang. At first
seeing the tall thin man on the undersized horse of less than 15 hands tall
and only about 900 pounds made for friendly needling, but they soon
had to appreciate the quick moves the horse made when herding he
larger Trotters.

Adolf became thoughtful as he watched the Mustang's surefooted
movements and the quickness the gelding was able to switch directions.
He told Oskar, "Why it don't seem like Slim does anything at all. His

horse is doing all the work. Slim could be sound asleep for all we know."

Slim told them some of the educated Texas ranchers had told him the mustangs had been in North America since the days of Columbus and enhanced by the early day Conquistadors such as Cortez. A traveling professor had told him that the word "mustang" meant stray or feral animal. He even said he had been told some were descendants to something called Bard horses.

Slim went on to tell them, "The cattlemen in Texas are copying the Comanche, the Shoshoni and the Ne Perce Indians in their breeding of the mustang. Their size and quickness are traits that work well with working cattle."

Even Oskar perked his head up to listen. He knew that anything Adolf chose to pay attention to meant something.

Slim went on to mention, "A bunch of ranchers have picked up the practice of breeding some Quarter horses with the little fellows and finding the offspring to have more strength and endurance."

Oskar could see that Adolf was deep in thought as he headed for his bunk after one lengthy discussion. He didn't prod Adolf. He knew his longtime friend was thinking and would eventually tell him after all the kinks were worked out. Adolf spent several days in silent thought.

As Oskar was waiting for Adolf to tell him his thoughts, Sven moved back to the bunk house and started regaining his incredible strength by working with the heavy hammer pounding iron. Oskar came up to Adolf one evening and asked, "Have you noticed Sven and Neale are still taking walks together in the evenings?"

"Yup," replied Adolf.

Oskar watched the walking pair for a while and then a big grin spread across his freckled face, "You don't think?"

"Yup."

"Well I'll be hog tied and trussed up like a Thanksgiving turkey." Oskar rapped Adolf across his broad shoulders and said, "Dang, now that is just damn neat."

That night Adolf surprised Oskar when he asked Slim, "Do you know where those wild mustangs hang out."

Slim rubbed his chin with a hand and squinted his eyes near shut, deep in thought, "I hear tell there is a whole bunch in them Arizona and Nevada territories, but I also know for a fact there is some west of the Great Plains around the southern Wyoming and northwest Kansas territories."

Oskar was convinced his thoughtful buddy had some new idea scrambling around in his bonnet like bees in a hive.

The next evening when Sven came back from his walk, Adolf asked his two friends to join him in the hayloft of the colt barn. Oskar grinned and said, "Now you ain't got some funny stuff in mind."

Recalling the young Mormon girl, Sally, Adolf sent a dark look that wiped Oskar's grin right off his face like a rainstorm on a dusty buckboard.

Adolf waited until his two mates were situated. Then he began talking like he had a prepared speech, "I like it on the Slash N, but you both know this is not the end game for me."

They nodded without interrupting their normally quiet leader, for they knew he was a deep thinker.

"Slim's little horse has got me to thinking." He took off his hat and wiped the inside band with his hand. "I like working with Trotters, but I think there is another future out there." After a short silence, Adolf continued, "I am hankering to go see those mustangs in the Kansas and Wyoming territories. Would also like to see them Rocky Mountains everybody talks about."

It got real quiet as the other two didn't know what to say. Where was Adolf driving this wagon? Did he think mustangs would make good Trotters?

Adolf got real serious and said, "I'm going to take a looksee at the mountains and the mustangs. I would like you two to come along."

Oskar didn't hesitate more than a couple of breaths before saying, "I'll go. I am kind of restless to see what's out yonder and those wild mountains everyone talks about."

Sven got real quiet and started fidgeting like ants were biting his butt. He took his hat off and ran a plate sized hand through his yellow hair. His face turned red and he kept his eyes down as he said, "Guys I'm real torn. We are powerful buddies and I hanker to trail along with you, but I really am hankering to be with Neale and plan to ask her to marry me when I have something to offer her."

Adolf slapped Sven's ham-like knee and spoke again, "That's what I'm thinking about. I want Caroline to come here and be my wife, but I have to build a future for us." He grinned at his buddies as he continued, "What if we start up our own ranch raising a new breed from these mustangs and quarter-horse mix?" He got a twinkle in his eye and said, "Someday there are going to be cattle ranches and farms where the buffalo run. I think there will be a need for horses to work those beefs. We could get ahead of the race and be ready for it to come to us."

Both friends looked into Adolf's eyes and saw that Adolf had a dream. "I think cattle are going to be a big thing. The people out east are going to need them to feed all the immigrants coming to America. I think we can get in on the beginning of a new thing. There is going to be a demand someday for better cattle ponies and I think Slim's pony will meet that need."

Oskar was dumbfounded. That was one of the longest speeches he had heard from Adolf, ever. He knew his friend was onto something, but just wasn't sure what it was yet.

Sven asked, "You think?"

"Someday they're going to settle them Great Plains. Think of the opportunity for us and our families. What you guys think?"

Sven said, "Ya betcha, I like it. But I gotta talk to Neale and find her leanings."

Adolf spoke up, "That's good. I would like to be moving out by next Saturday." Then he thought a bit and said, "Sven, talk to Neale tomorrow and I'll have a chat with Uncle Gottlieb. Sure hope he doesn't get mad. He has helped us an awful lot. This will leave him mighty shorthanded."

All sat quiet, even the normal chatty Oskar. All had mixed up feelings, torn between chasing the elephant and loyalty to the Slash N.

Chapter 16

A beautiful summer day went unnoticed by Adolf as he nervously walked to Uncle Gottlieb's office. His uncle was browsing through a stack of papers with a feather quill pen in his hand. "We should have a good crop of foals this summer," remarked Gottlieb. Seeing the serious look on Adolf's face, he put the pen down and leaned back in his chair.

"Why do you look like a kicked dog?" Uncle Gottlieb was very concerned, "Plop your butt in a chair and tell me what's got your shorts in a bind."

Adolf set his hat on the desk, being right careful not to upset the inkwell or scatter horse records. Turning the chair backwards, he leaned forward with his arms hugging the chair back. He nervously looked into his uncle's eyes and cleared the frogs from his throat, "Ummm, Uncle Gottlieb, you been darn good to us and all three of us are downright grateful to you."

Then Adolf started speaking about the mustang horses and spelling out his thoughts and ideas. As he talked his excitement shoved the shyness aside and filled the room with the hopes and visions of this thoughtful young man.

As Adolf reached the stopping point of his dream, the nervousness pranced back in and he started stuttering and wondering if his words sounded like a fool kid writing his first Christmas letter to Santa.

Uncle Gottlieb leaned forward and put on a serious face before talking. "Adolf, I always knew you were a smart one. Your ideas reminds me of your dad and me when we were first pulling on long pants." He somehow altered his face to reflect pride. "This world grows because of dreams. Those that have the gumption to chase them, now those are the doers."

He leaned back and folded his arms behind his head with a face of thoughtfulness. "You know that your grand pappy raised them big ole Belgium draft horses in Pennsylvania. He got the idea that they would replace both the Percherons and the oxen as the big muscle for hauling wagons and for farming. That was okay for brothers Heiner and Ruben, but your daddy and I had other dreams. We had watched the Trotters races at get-togethers in Maine and Kentucky and those Trotters got under our skin."

Uncle Gottlieb's face got younger as his eyes were looking way back to his bringing ups. "We'd stay up deep into the night and trade dreams. Before long we took off to Ohio and got a job with old man Alvin Dobler training Trotters. We saved up all our knowledge and money and a few years later had that ranch your daddy and momma has now. Pa pitched in some seed money, which sure did help get us started.

"I read a news print about them Ozark Trotters getting started. Sure did scratch my interest, so I came out here. I have never looked back, no sir." Then he leaned onto his desk and smiled. "I knew this was just a rest in your trail. Figured you would move on someday, and now is as good as tomorrow."

Finally, Adolf spoke again, "This is sure going to leave you short-handed."

"Been there before and will again. That is none of your concern." Uncle Gottlieb came around the table to take Adolf into his loving embrace. "I know your pappy, my brother Olaf, will be plumb proud of his youngest. I sure am."

After supper Adolf and Oskar were sitting on a spot of grass by the barn chewing on blades of grass. Oskar was chatting with excitement as they waited for Sven to return from his habitual walk with Neale. Adolf was only half listening, sorting out the few meaningful pieces of Oskar's run-on mouth. Adolf's thoughts were far out in the future fitting pieces of the unknown puzzle together.

"You guys there?" Sven's words interrupted both Adolf's dreams and Oskar's crow like chatter.

Oskar recovered first, or at least, spoke first, "How did that come off?"

Sven dropped beside his buddies with a quizzical look. "It was right out confusing. Sure hard to read signs on women. It is perplexing."

Oskar burst out laughing as he swatted the big guy on one oversized shoulder, "Hell man, everybody knows that is a sure enough fact."

Adolf just grunted.

"I hemmed and hawed about our going west after mustangs and she didn't say a damned thing. Hell, her face didn't even alter. If I didn't know better, I would have thought she was deaf." Sven took his hat off and shook about a pint of sweat from it before he continued, "She just sat there making me real jittery. I felt like a virgin on wedding night."

Sven used his red bandanna to wipe his damp forehead that just beaded back up with drops of sweat. "I got scared and damned if I didn't blurt out that I loved her and planned to marry her. I don't know what came over me. It wasn't in my plan to say that."

Sven stared into his companion's eyes, "You know what she did?" Without giving either a chance to respond he went on, "Ufta, it's damn crazy. She started crying and I was real scared I had upset her. Then she threw her arms around this young Swedish neck and planted about a hundred kisses full on my lips. I was sure confused, but then she said - *'You big dumb bloke. Sure took you long enough. I thought I was going to have to do the asking.'* Now doesn't that beat all?"

Adolf shook his friend's gigantic hand. For one of the few times Adolf could remember, Oskar had nothing to say. With tears in his eyes, Ozkar took hold of Sven's other hand and held on.

Chapter 17

The summer sun was taking a sneak peek above the eastern edge of the earth and thinking seriously about becoming morning, but the day for Adolf and his troop had already started. Nervous excitement was competing with fear of the unknown as Adolf, Oskar, and Sven prepared for the new day. This was the day, the day for riding away from the comfort of the Slash N and into whatever future was waiting to the west.

Although it was only 5:30, the entire Slash N cast was watching the three young men's preparation. Shifting from foot to foot were the three hired hands in addition to the tight grouping of the Nagel family. Adolf's relatives had surprised the three ex-employees yesterday, not only with a barbeque, but with special gifts. All three had each been given a Missouri mule as a pack animal.[vii]

All five members of the Missouri Nagel family had pitched in for the sixty dollars to buy the three mules. The young travelers were struck dumb and were sure they knew where Santa actually lived and it wasn't the North Pole.

As he presented the young men with these large draft mules, Uncle Gottlieb told them, "You're gonna be crossing the Great American Desert. Why, there ain't a settlement much less a town that whole way to the Mountains. Won't be nowhere to supply up, not even a white pioneer to borrow from. You got to carry all you'll need except meat. All of them wild buffalos will provide plenty of that."

The mood was very solemn, emphasized by Neale's long face with tears flowing freely. She hovered behind Sven, with both arms grasping him possessively.

Shorty had his hands tucked in his belt behind his back with his head looking at the ground as he tried to hide the wetness on his cheeks. The only person with a smile was Slim. He was wishing he was going with the boys to roundup mustangs. He also felt prideful that the idea had sprouted from the seed of his tales.

The three were packed and ready to set out, but no one knew how to break away. Uncle Gottlieb moved the ball by going to each young man to thank them for their service and wish them success. Ailish followed on his heels and handed each man a gunny sack filled with fresh bread, biscuits, and huge beef sandwiches. Then she not only gave each a long hug, but also a wet kiss on the cheek. Like their father, Henry and Bill thanked them, shook their hand firmly, and patted their shoulders as they extended their wishes for success.

One by one, Timothy, Shorty, and Slim stepped forward to give their individual wishes for success and backslaps. Shorty also gave each his own bashful man-hug. Finally, Neale let go of Sven and gave Adolf and Oskar a long hug and a kiss on the cheek. Afterward, she immediately went back to grab hold of Sven's hand. Sven and Neale kissed unashamedly. Then Sven joined the other two in climbing onto the saddle. Waves continued until the three were out of sight, then Mrs. Nagel put her arms around her bawling daughter. The men all stood with their hands in their pockets, deep in their own private thoughts.

The riders led their pack mules around the east side of the S shaped Lake Ozark before turning north west toward the fledging towns of Westport Landing and Village of Kansas, which marked the spot on the Missouri River in the Missouri Territory to meet up with the Santa Fe Trail.

Surprisingly Oskar stayed inside himself. It was Sven who started talking first – babbling about Adolf's wonderful female cousin and his love for her. That brought Oskar out of his thoughts a little. He agreed with Sven's assessment of Neale's attributes and told him that he knew how much Neale loved Sven and how well they were matched.

Then, like someone had turned a page of a book, Sven changed the subject to the quest. The mood of all three young men perked up. Oskar and Sven competed for the chattiest sidekick award and Adolf pitched in periodically to provide missing information. Mostly, Adolf rode with a smile forming on his face as he listened to the magpie-like exchanges. By the approach of evening, all three men had set aside the previous dark mood and embraced a boy-like thirst for adventure.

The next morning it was a tossup between Oskar's chipmunk chatter and the barking of mule farts. It didn't matter the winner because the sight of the lake was just awesome. It even quieted Oskar for a while. Sven said he thought looking south along tree-lined Taylor Falls up in Minnesota was a pleasure to the eye, but this sure beats all. The only negative of the experience was the need to look out for Osage warriors. They were headed for the Osage River, which meant they were traipsing through the hunting land of the Osage Nation.

Reaching the river, they saw that its meandering nature allowed for many crossing choices with the numerous sand bars. The spring runoff was done. They were thankful, because they knew it would be impossible to forge during flood stage. It also allowed them to turn northwest towards the Missouri River.

Chapter 18

Sven, Oskar, and Adolf were giving their horses and mules a break on a grassy hilltop looking down onto the mighty Missouri. They lounged against the packs, gazing at the rushing water below, content in swatting at blue blowflies slowly drifting around the cheese they were lunching on. These flies were no bother, not like the biting deer flies they fought last evening or the larger, hungry horse flies. Horse flies didn't just bite, they took chunks of flesh from any exposed skin, animal or human. These blowflies were not troublesome at all.

More bothersome than the blowflies was the Missouri humidity. Sven announced, "Couldn't get more soaked if it was raining. The air is damn full of water."

Oskar decided not to be out-complained, so added, "Damn glad I can swim. Never knew it was needed on dry land."

Adolf suggested, "Let's go down there and wash the stink out of our clothes and off our bodies." So they did. After which they packed up and followed the river west.

Riding steady, Sven said, "Been noticing some pig farms by sight and smell. Even saw some patches of knee high corn here and there."

"We're getting right close to Westport Landing," Adolf told the others. "Thought we would stop and listen for talk of Indians in that Great Plain land mass."

Two days later they topped a tree covered hill and saw a scruffy settlement. It consisted of mostly unpainted, rough-cut lumber, a scattering of log buildings, and numerous canvas tents oiled to slow the rain seepage. The smell of burning wood went hand in hand with smoke pretending to be little clouds rising from various buildings.

They led their top-loaded mules down the widest and most rutted street, which meandered between the largest structures. Oskar laughed, "Do you see all them buildings bunched together? Look it all the unused space around. Why don't they spread out instead of crowding each other?"

Sven was chuckling also as he spoke his mind, "Sure is no St. Louis." Then he said, "Why look at all the ways them people are dressed. Must be some sort of costume party."

Westport Landing had started to attract fur traders in buckskin, along with farmers in bibbed overalls and city folk in suits and ties. Even some stray army gents in blue woolen uniforms were onsite along. The women were in work dresses or Sunday type clothes.

Oskar asked, "How the hell do they think of all them there different types of stores? Why there are even two churches! Do they each have their own God?"

Adolf was a little embarrassed of his two sidekicks open mouthed gawking. He grumped, "Why not just carry a sign telling everyone we are green pilgrims?" Then he stopped Buck and asked, "What you think of us stopping at this general store and stocking up on ammunition? We are going to need extra rifle rounds to shoot Bison and lead balls, powder and percussion caps for our pistols to fight off Indians if they attack us."

Sven and Oskar were somewhat subdued, but still snuck glances at the sights as they dismounted. They tied the horses and mules to the tie posts. Then they all stretched the kinks out before entering the store. Oskar elbowed Sven behind Adolf's back and nodded his head at the women's undergarments in plain view of everyone. They both put a hand over their mouths to conceal little boy chuckles.

A skinny man with a stomach paunch and wire spectacles, wearing a shirt with one of them detachable celluloid collars and some woman's apron, came over and asked, "May I help you gentlemen." Oskar chuckled and pretended to be looking for gentlemen, until Adolf's elbow left a dent in his side.

With the help of the skinny store clerk, the three found a good many supplies. In addition to the ammunition, Adolf piled up a couple sacks of flour, a sack of beef jerky, four more canteens, a couple bags of hard tack, three long gray slickers, and a large bag of various flavored jawbreakers. The store clerk loaned them a couple boxes to carry the purchases out to their mules. After splitting the load amongst the three packs, they started leading their animals down the street. A conscious effort was made not to step in the piles of horse apples sprouting up from the street.

Sven brought the boys short when he said, "There's a saloon. Sure could taste a beer."

Oskar looked over and seconded Sven's suggestion with, "Now that is one damn good idea!" He took hold of Adolf's arm and pleaded, "Aw, come on. It's going to be a long dry spell to them far away mountain settlement places."

Both Sven and Oskar pretended to fall down with surprise when Adolf smiled and said, "Why not?"

Oskar's joking around had placed him in front of a wobbling man coming out of the saloon. He was decked out in greasy buckskin outfit with some dead animal on his head, probably once a coon's skin cap. The man was looking at his feet and walked right into Oskar. Oskar was quick enough to keep the man from falling but didn't have any skills for keeping the stink from slapping the young men like a fly swatter. It was damn nauseating.

The man was not only covered in grease and what appeared to be the dried innards of animals, but his hair and beard were competing in a shaggy contest and seemed alive with vermin. Fumes of alcohol were not enough to hide the stench of his foul breath. The combination of all those competing smells brought Oskar and his friends to the thought of puking. The man recovered, but he glared at Oskar while expelling spit as well as words, "Why the hell don't yah look where you're stomping your feet?"

Then he took a swing at Oskar which Oskar ducked. Smiling he said, "My fault ole timer. I should pay more attention." Then he turned to walk toward the open saloon door.

The skin clad man huffed, pulled out an Arkansas toothpick, and advanced towards Oskar. Before he could take a second step, a hand the size of a shovel grasped his shirt and lifted him plumb off the street before dumping him into a fresh pile of horseshit, which may have improved his stink. Sven glared at the man, waved a fence post sized finger then turned to follow Oskar.

The angry man was still holding his knife and pulled it back to throw, but the click of a pistol hammer cocking froze him mid movement. Looking over to where the sound came from, he was looking into the black hole of Adolf's Colt Paterson. Mr. Stinky sobered up like he was thrown in a lake. He started to put the long blade back in his belt, but the shake of Adolf's head suggested otherwise and he just dropped it before scampering down the street.

Adolf put his .36 back in his holster before picking up the knife. He looked at it and then dropped it in a saddlebag. Four grizzled codgers were whittling sticks on a bench by the door and giggling like little boys putting chalk dust on the chair of their teacher. One elected himself their spokesman and told Adolf, "You boys sure enough teached that bison skinner."

Another one spoke up, "Don't you worry 'bout your stuff. We're set to be here till too dark to see and will watch over it. We are pleased for the entertainment." Adolf tipped two fingers to his hat brim and followed his buddies.

Adolf stepped out of the doorway to let his eyes adjust to the dingy room. He spotted the two at a table on the right side with four full mugs of beer topped with a couple inches of white suds and two mugs most empty. The suds from the empty mugs were dripping from upper lips, beneath grins reminiscent of boys licking their mom's cake mix bowl.

"Where you been?" chirped Oskar. "Thought we was going have to drink your two beers before they melted." Sven seemed to find this funny as he giggled and wiped the back of his hand across his grin.

A chubby bartender with muttonchops brought them four more mugs and collected four nickels. He swiped a mostly dry rag through the rings on the table. In a friendly tone to build business, he asked if they were new to the landing. Oskar told him they were just traveling through to the mountains.

After he walked away humming some music off key, one of the mule skinners at the next table scooted his chair towards the boys and with a friendly smile spoke up, "Couldn't help hearing you say you were riding into the Nation territories."

Adolf looked at the burly driver and then to his equally husky tablemate. Both had sleeves rolled to their elbows, uncovering forearms the size of four by fours with hair. "If you're familiar with that area, we would welcome any insight. Join us for a beer?" He slid two of the fresh mugs towards the men and they both brought their chairs over. The men introduced themselves as Gus Clemens and Cootie Hatcher. They were indeed mule skinners for the Hawkens and Sons Freight Line out of the neighboring Village of Kansas. They all got a chuckle because old man Hawkens wasn't even married and there sure weren't any legitimate sons to make the name true like.

Cootie said, "Clem Hawkens says the company name makes the company seem family like." This, of course, gave the five conversationalists a beer induced hoot.

After a few minutes of creating a buddy type relationship, Cootie got serious and asked, "You do know that there are thousands of Indians in that Kansas Territory?" The boys shook their heads, flinging some beer from their chins, like a coon hound shaking rain water from its loose skin. The two freight drivers looked at each other with some trepidation.

Not to be outdone on giving information, Gus butted right on in, "Ya got the Apache, Comanche, Delaware, Cherokee, and Chippewa, I know of for true."

Cootie jumped back in the conversation when Gus took a swallow of beer, "Plus mostly peaceful Arapaho and Cheyenne. The government just done pushed the eastern Fox, Illinois, and Iroquois folks west of the Mississippi. And whoever else's lifetime treaties they decide to forfeit."

Gus wetted the back of his hand from his chin whiskers and took his turn, "Now most all of them tribes are buffalo followers. And those big ole beasts do keep moving to find new grass to harvest."

When Gus hesitated to take in some air, Cootie ventured out, "Most the young bucks are always looking to take coup, lift scalps, and steal horses. Nothing impresses them flirty Injun maidens more."

Both harmonized like they had practiced a duet, "It right out dangerous through that tall grass lands."

Gus' eyes got round as he thought of something else, "The bison are so big that they don't even know to be afraid. Mostly they will leave yah alone, but they can be ornery and, if they are, they are a real fright. A ton of pure muscle with horns that will gut your horse before you can say scat. If they stampede, you'll only be grease spots on their hooves." With another thought he added, "Got to keep a look out for twisters, wind walls, and lightening blasting thunder storms too. It sure is not a Sunday social out there."

As the three friends left the saloon to head westward, they had a lot of new worries on their minds. Each young man was in his own thoughts but shared the same question - W*ere their drinking friends just funning them?* All three arrived at a common answer – they may have been funning a little, but most of what they'd said was sound advice.'

Chapter 19

The sky this early summer morning was a brilliant, pure blue without a show of white in sight. To the north, west, and south, this tapestry of blue was resting on a green carpet of swaying splendor. Not a third color was in sight. Adolf imagined it was like looking out over the ocean from the Mayflower. It was a damn different type of view, but probably the most beautiful sight he had ever laid eyes on. Well, it was the most beautiful other than Caroline, of course.

"Gosh almighty. Would yah look at that?" Oskar's chin almost hit the pommel of his saddle as he flat-out gawked at his first viewing of the Great Plains of America. As far as they could see was a sea of waist tall grass waving in ripples as it tried to catch the summer breeze. The continual motion of the prairie made it seem alive, like it was breathing.

Everybody they had talked to referred to the Great Plains as flat, just a wasteland of nothing They could see it just wasn't so. At first glance it may appear flat, but the land was a constant rolling. Dips would fall off and ridges would rise up on the horizon. As they rode they could see bluffs in the distance and found gullies created from erosion, both wind and water. Even the long grasses were not flat. There were different kinds of grasses at different heights, not large differences but not straight across either. Some grasses were four feet high, although most were over six, and there was a variation in color. From a distance, it all blended together into a solid green, but the constant wind made it ripple as if it was one large living organism.

Sven was spellbound as he threw in his observation, "Not a tree out there. I would of never believed it."

Adolf was quiet as usual, but this time it was because of understanding the true magnitude of God and his creations. He just wanted to etch this view into his mind to keep until eternity.

As if reading his thoughts Oskar whispered, "Sure would like to capture this picture to hang on my wall someday." Adolf looked over at Oskar and nodded his head. He felt thankful that his two friends were here to share this. He knew he didn't have words to describe this well enough for anyone else to understand.

Sven said, "Too bad it's so early in the day. I'd try to talk you into camping here to look at this all day long."

His remarks seemed to bring back reality to the men, so one by one they drifted out into this tall wonder. Looking back, their passageway seemed to be an act of irreverence marring the prairie.

At noon they stopped beside a pond that was a perfect circle about thirty feet across. The pond was only about two feet deep but the bottom was solid, not muddy, and the water was cool and refreshing. Sven spoke up after doing some study, "This looks to be man-made. Never seen acts of nature so exact-like."

Adolf looked closer and dragged his hand along the bottom, "Feel that. There appears to be bits of hair pressed into the bottom." Then he looked up with a smile on his face. "I've read about this. This is a buffalo wallow. They can be hundreds of years in the making. The bison lay on the ground to rub off insects. Their tufts of hair mix with the grass and dirt to become like adobe. Rain water is trapped to form this pond because the adobe-like bottom allows no leakage."

All three of these young boys were book educated. They went to school until they got big enough to work and then their moms kept teaching them at home. They had already agreed that their favorite books were the James Fennimore Cooper series including *The Last of the Mohicans, The Pathfinder, The Deerslayer, and The Pioneers.* Adolf read anything he could lay his hands on, while the other two admitted they were more of the once-in-a-while variety of reader.

After loosening the cinches on the saddles and taking the packs off the mules, the young men took out some jerky and hardtack out of their saddlebags to chow down on for lunch. The horses and mules seemed to enjoy the tall, juicy prairie grass that was there in abundance. The water was wonderful from the buffalo wallow, and they emptied all their canteens and refilled from the pond.

After the young men and their animals had drunk their fill, they loaded up and started west again. Like some magic act, the sky changed rapidly: white clouds were chased by huge grey clouds, then distant thunder rumbled toward them to be joined by sky-filling jagged streaks of lightning. At Adolf's suggestion, they dismounted to put on their new slickers and grab some oiled canvas sheets to tent over their animals. Quarter sized drops of rain splashed against their faces before they could get under the canvas with their animals. To the west a solid sheet of dark gray was running toward them. Quickly the clouds arrived and water dumped from the sky as if giants were throwing giant-sized buckets of it at them.

It got even louder under the tent-like structure, as the rain attacked more viciously. They had to hold all six animals steady because they wanted to run from this unknown enemy. Suddenly, like the pump had gone dry, it just stopped. Not even a sprinkle was left. When they peeked out, the dark wall was way to the east and the blue sky was back in place.

Oskar, being the first always to interrupt the silence, laughed and observed, "Sure don't have to fret none about water. Every buffalo wallow in the Great Plains should be brim full."

Sven spoke up, "I've never seen mother nature to be so fickle my whole life. That was the fastest change of weather I ever did see." Then he grinned, "Think it will snow before nightfall?" He bent over laughing at his own joke. Even stern Adolf had to chuckle and Oskar added his own knee slapping laughter.

They came upon another smaller wallow about dusk time, so decided to make camp. After watering, unpacking, and staking the animals on long tethers, they grabbed their short shovels and dug a fire pit. The pit was edged out about ten feet on all sides to keep from catching the grass on fire. Then they grabbed handfuls of the long grass and twisted them into tight bundles to burn. Before long, they were slurping hot coffee and supping on German sausages, fried tatters in grease, and boiled beans.

Tuckered out from the long day and new experiences, they laid out their homemade bedrolls, blankets sewed to a canvas mat, on top of layers of soft grass and gazed up at the millions of stars overhead. Before long they were all asleep.

Chapter 20

It had been a couple days since the torrential rainstorm. They had spotted a few Indians on horseback twice and this morning had watched a staggered line of about fifty, including women and children, with pony-pulled travois carrying their household goods. A couple of the younger men rode over with an older brave who was sporting a feathered bonnet trailing to the back of his spotted pony and carrying a flint-pointed spear in his left hand. When the boys all raised their right hand with palm facing outward, the older Indian did the same. Following the greeting, the group of Indians returned to their people.

Adolf announced to his friends, "Buffalo must be close. They're following a herd."

The white men looked over the tall grass and waved when several of the young ones stopped to gawk and wave at them.

Oskar said, "Seem friendly. Wonder what tribe they are?"

Just before high noon the three travelers came on their first change of scenery. The grass was only about an inch tall. Here and there were clumps of taller blades left untouched, but not many. It looked like an army of elves had marched through swinging scythes and another bunch had raked the fallen grass and carried it all away. Gray dots were splattered throughout like checkers on the biggest board ever. Buffalo chips in the multitude told a tale of grazing bison. A harvested strip about two miles wide ran north to south, never ending.

Oskar shook his head and proclaimed, "Now that is a beginning to end natural process. Grass grows, is eaten, and then fertilized to grow again. Momma Nature is downright smart."

The four-legged travelers were given a break to munch on the tall Blue Stemmed grass. The young men joined along by munching on jerky and hardtack, washed down with cool water from their canteens. Lazing in the warming sun was appreciated by all nine critters. There was something about sticking a long blade of moist grass in your mouth, putting hands behind your head and contemplating the blue sky that made the three men enjoy being alive. Oskar wasn't content with the silence, "This is the life. Ain't it boys?"

Feeling obligated to reply, Sven answered, "Beats working, it surely does."

Adolf added his normal part to the conversation by staying silent. His mind was busy thinking about making his dreams come to fruition. He could see herds of wild mustangs foaling a new breed of working ponies. His dream included having Caroline and his two friends by his side as their future materialized.

Later, as they rode across the wide open bareness, they started to feel uneasy. If they could see forever, so could scalp happy Indian warriors. Adolf took notice that both Oskar and Sven were twisting their heads in all directions in search for danger. He felt tiny spiders crawling up and down his spine, reflecting that he was also imagining being put upon by copper skinned heathens. Every distant movement set his imagination into action. Because of his natural characteristic of planning ahead, he found that he was inventing defensive responses in his mind. He considered looking for buffalo wallows to fight from or fighting from behind the bodies of their four legged companions. He found that he was damn anxious to get back into that tall grass over yonder. Of course they would still stand out above the grass, but it felt less visible than out here in the naked space.

When they reached the far side of the short grass, he heard both his buddies blow out held in breath like a tea kettle reaching boil. He knew he was no different when he wiped the sweat off his brow and shifted forward in his saddle. He realized that Oskar's chattering had long been absent, when Oskar started his meaningless, but welcomed, babble. It just plain seemed a relief to hear that babble in the background, like birds starting to sing after an angry bear passed by. Adolf forced himself to relax and was again content to listen to the summer breeze use the long grass to serenade them with nature's own music.

Adolf tuned into Oskar's chatter when it changed tone and rhythm. "Look up ahead! The grass is a dark brown. I have never seen that before."

A ways out yonder it was sure enough a dark brown, but it was not dancing to the breeze. Instead, parts were moving and other patches were not. Was this some trick of nature?

Sven bellowed, "It ain't grass. It looks to me to be large shaggy cows. Ufta! That's them wild buffalo, you betcha."

Here was another awesome sight of nature. As they drifted closer, the size of the herd seemed to grow. It was not just huge; it covered miles in all directions. About a hundred yards out, movement to their left grabbed their attention. Hawk feathers waving in the breeze in concert with the tall grass were displayed on about thirty copper-skinned, shirtless men with long black hair. They were astride ponies covered with various designs from red handprints and white stripes to yellow copies of the sun.

All but two were gazing at the tons of meat shortening the tall grass one bite at a time. Those remaining two were more remarkable only because they were looking at the three white men. They were showing neither fear nor anger, only a majestic look of interest. Half of the braves held stone-tipped long spears with bows on their backs and quivers of arrows on their hips. The rest of the hunters, for hunters they were, held their bows in their hands with arrows already notched. Although most were wearing one to three foot-long feathers sticking straight up, two had headdress bonnets trailing feathers all down their backs, and one was wearing a hat made from the head of a horned buffalo.

Suddenly, the one wearing the buffalo head yelled a high pitch yodel and dug into his pony with his heels to jump it into the herd. Like the shot signaling the start of a race, his action set all into motion. With the same highpitched sound, all were into the herd throwing spears or shooting arrows. The biggest surprise was that, at first, the majority of buffalo did not acknowledge this death-dealing attack. Then some of the most aware lumbered into a ground covering run, but stopped as soon as the Indian attack stopped. It appeared that close to one hundred dead brown beasts were lying on the ground with spears and arrows attached. Most of the buffalo were dead, but the few that were alive were being shot again by the returning riders.

The hunters tilted their heads towards the heavens and raised arms to the sky. Their chanting was similar to people praying to God to give thanks for their meal. When the chanting stopped, a higher pitched warble erupted from women and children who rushed out of hiding and descended on the carcasses like ants to a fallen sparrow. A well-practiced butchering began as the bodies were gutted, skinned and hacked into various hunks of meat piled on the buffalo hides. The men did not participate in the butchering. They rode into the tall grass and returned with pack animals with some type of carrying structure on their backs and trailing long limbed travois. Several dogs also were dragging travois. The men watched in groups, talking excitably and exhibiting hand gestures reminiscent of fishermen exchanging exaggerations of their accomplishments as the women and children packed the meat.

As the group disappeared into the tall grass all that was left were bones lying amongst fresh buffalo chips. Even that picture disappeared as the massive herd spread over the killing ground leaving Adolf and his friends with only their memories. The last of the Indians to leave were the two that had looked at the three white riders. They sought them out again and raised their bows over their heads and waved as if they were departing friends.

Chapter 21

Adolf suggested they shoot and butcher one of the buffalo to provide fresh meat and the decision became unanimous. Adolf pulled out the large bore Hawkens and knelt on the ground. From a hundred and fifty yards away, he aimed behind the ear of a large bull. Although the blast was like an exploding volcano, the only movement by the herd was the bull collapsing. The cow next to him flinched with a shiver of her skin but didn't even raise her head.

Adolf reloaded and Oskar held his Kentucky rifle in front of him. The huge herd showed no awareness of them, much less any aggression. The men were still very nervous about being amongst so many of these oversized animals. Sven pulled a heavy broad ax and a butcher knife from his pack. He sharpened both using a whetstone he always carried and proceeded to dismember the bull in the same fashion he had butchered livestock on his parents' Minnesota homestead. Although he was very experienced, it was clear to all that he was neither as fast nor efficient as the Indian women.

Bringing all three mules to the mound of fresh meat that was still dripping blood, they consolidated the current loads onto two mules. Copying the Indian women, they wrapped the meat in the buffalo hide and placed the four hundred pounds on the back of the remaining mule. Unlike the Indians, they left most of the intestines and the head with the bones. They did remember to cut out the tongue, which the freighters had told them was delicious. After a very short discussion, they also took the brain. Although none professed to want to try eating it, they remembered it was good for curing the hide.

Adolf asked Sven, "Are you familiar with preparing the hide?" Getting a positive response he added, "That will be great for the upcoming cold winter. We need two more."

"You betcha," Sven agree. "We need to have bed robes to sleep warm and comfy."

Oskar chuckled, "Would like to cuddle under one with a willing woman to keep me warm."

Adolf and Sven rolled their eyes and groaned. They had already picked out their future wives and were not on the prowl like Oskar.

Buffalo were not the only eatables they noticed - mule deer, white tail deer, pronghorns, large elk, and long-eared jackrabbits and smaller cotton tails. There were also plenty of mean badgers, smelly skunks, waddling porcupines, and red and gray fox. Each night they were serenaded by coyotes singing boasts to the moon.

Above them the sky almost appeared black when the flying animal kingdom crossed the sky, including: snow geese, Canadian honkers, and all types of duck. Pheasants, grouse and prairie hens popped out of the grass only to disappear again. Of course, all types of smaller birds took to wing like puffs of smoke. Several kinds of hawk - swain, red tail, and cooper - cruised above, peering down for smaller meals scurrying in the grass. Higher up were their cousins, the golden and bald eagles, majestically looking over their prairie kingdom.

It was proving difficult to take in all of the sights on display, but Adolf drew rein to his gray and pointed to the northwest, "Ain't those trees?"

In the distance appeared tops of trees. "Sure enough," Oskar verified, "What do you think?"

"From the looks, I bet a river or creek," Adolf announced, "Let's take a peek."

As they got closer it became clearer that there were indeed large trees ahead. They were concentrating on this new sight and almost failed to notice movement to the left, but only almost. All three jerked their heads to observe movement above the tall grass on the horizon. Definitely not a single animal, it was a large group of copper-skinned men riding parallel.

"Make a run for those trees," Adolf commanded. It had not taken him but a moment to see these Indians were different from the ones they'd seen hunting. This was a party of about thirty or more warriors, without women or children. This seemed much more dangerous. That feeling was soon confirmed. The war party stopped, looked at them, and then charged them at full gallop. Distant sounds of high-pitched whooping outdistanced the Indians to reach the ears of the non-Indians, sending shivers of fear up their backs. This was a war party intent on taking scalps – theirs.

The race was on. Scared but determined, Adolf and crew knew they could reach the trees first. They were closer, plus their long-legged horses were faster. Even the slower mules were damn fast, and if not fast enough they could be easily cut loose by just dropping their leads.

Adolf was pretty sure if it came to that the mules would follow along anyway. They were accustomed to following the big horses. This proved to not be a concern. They were riding across a large flood plain that separated the tall grass from the mostly cotton wood trees. Old cotton wood trees stood fifty foot tall amongst hundreds of their fallen ancestors. Elm, ash, and willow were scattered amongst them.

Adolf rode past the first trees and jumped off his gelding. He quickly led Buck and the trailing mule about thirty yards deeper into a nice group of ancient trees. There he tied the horses to underbrush, and pulled both the Hawkens and the ten gauge out of their sheaths. He also grabbed his war bag with ammunition from behind his saddle. Oskar and Sven duplicated Adolf and all three ran back to the first line of trees. Some of these mammoths were almost five feet across. He plopped down behind a dead trunk four foot high lying at the base of a giant of a cottonwood.

The Indians were still riding in the tall grass, not yet reaching the flood plain. Adolf assessed their selected fighting ground as he laid the big .54 caliber rifle on top of the dead cottonwood and leaned the long shotgun beside him. He opened the war bag and withdrew what he would need to reload each of his weapons.

The dead cottonwood grove extended thirty or more feet. While Adolf kept watch, Oskar and Sven rolled huge dead tree trunks to both the sides giving them a three-sided fort, then they returned alongside Adolf.

"Adolf you're the best long shot. Sven can reload the Kentucky Long Rifles and I'll reload your big Hawkens," said Oskar. Neither saw Sven's frown. He thought he was a pretty fair to middling shot himself.

But this was not the time to argue, so he added Oskar's Kentucky Long Rifle to his and laid out the powder, balls, and his ramrod.

The war party was charging out of the grass and heading onto the dried sandy flood plain, screaming as loud as they could. The front Indian was over four hundred yards out yet, so Sven was not prepared when Adolf's weapon roared to life. He was amazed to see a red smear explode on the rider's chest as he was knocked from his pony, no longer aware of his previous world.

He almost forgot to hand Adolf one of the Long Rifles. My God, he had never seen a shot anywhere near that distance in his young life. Still in a state of fascination, he again was not prepared when the sound of the Kentucky rifle barked. Through the cloud of rising black smoke the next Indian pony's chest blossomed red and it fell on its head. His rider threw his hands forward to stop his own fall. As he hit the ground, the pony completed a tail-over-head somersault and placed nine hundred pounds of dead horse on top of the brave. Adolf grabbed the third rifle out of the hand of the dazed Sven and fired towards targets that were now two hundred yards away. The leading brave's head exploded like a watermelon hit by a sledgehammer. Sven finally came to life and started reloading the two empty rifles Adolf had pitched to him.

The remaining Indians completed an about-face as perfect as any parade soldiers and reentered the green grass. It was very obvious they were as shocked as Sven. Three were dead and they had not gotten close enough to fire one arrow.

As wiser warriors yelled after them, five young riders ignored all warnings and galloped back out of the grass. They were spread in a wide line and leaning against their horses' necks to provide smaller targets. Adolf didn't fire until they were about three hundred yards away and then one of the Kentucky rifles roared again. Part of the left thigh of the center rider separated from the rest of his leg. His frightened paint pony reared, flinging his rider off his rump. Then the horse ran like he was being chased by a mountain lion heading anywhere but here. The remaining four Indians had reversed and were in hot pursuit of the riderless pony. They had just ridden by the most distant body, when Adolf's large .54 caliber Hawkens announced its superiority and blew the hindmost rider's left arm clear off.

Oskar spoke up, "Spooked? I have never known you to miss two shots like that."

Adolf didn't change facial expression as he answered, "Who said I missed either shot? They now have to use some of their warriors to take care of the wounded."

Birds returned to the grove after two hours and a couple of beavers returned to work. A fox ran out to the dead horse, but decided to wait a while longer. A long-legged blue heron glided in to land behind them in the river. Even songbirds started trying out for the choir. It was quite peaceful in the grove of trees as they watched the Indians in the distance. The braves were sure patient, even the poor bastard shot in the thigh who was lying out on the sand.

A decision had been made. The Indians became active. Five braves rode to the left and five more to the right, leaving six or seven where they were.

Adolf said, "They are going to try to come in from both sides." He ran his hand across his face and took off his hat to run his hand through his hair. Then he spoke up again, "Sven, take the shotgun and set up on the left. Leave the rifles with me."

Then he tapped Oskar on the shoulder, "Ole friend, take your revolver over to the right. It will be in close shooting. I'll stay here. I can protect the front with the rifles and cover both of you with my pistol. Keep your eyes to the river in case they try to come that way. That river is pretty wide so I don't reckon they'll hanker doing that."

No sound was heard, but Adolf figured it was close to time. He spotted some copper skin on Sven's right about twenty yards out. An arrow could be seen sticking out of the branches, but then the big ten gauge burped, very loudly. The copper skin disintegrated in a cloud of red meat and pieces of white bone, and the arrow fell straight down. Some dumb youngster let out a piercing war cry as he stepped from behind a tree only ten yards away and charged towards Sven. Before Adolf could react, the second barrel of the shotgun joined the fight. The whole front of the warrior was mangled flesh, he looked down in shock and horror before giving up the ghost.

Peeking around the giant tree on Oskar's side, Adolf was just in time to watch Oskar send another to the happy hunting ground. The sounds of panicked running resounded through brush, announcing braves in a hasty retreat.

They watched as three riders on Sven's side and four on Oskar's rode back to the waiting braves. Before too long the wounded brave out front started chanting. Adolf knew he was singing his death chant.

The tall grass parted and an older warrior walked out with his arms up and his palms facing forward. After a few minutes indecision, Adolf walked out with his palms facing the same. The older Indian walked out to the wounded brave and with surprising strength lifted the brave and carried him to the grass. Then he returned and held a spear with many feathers over his head. He took the spear in both hands and snapped it in half. He dropped to his knees and laid the broken spear on the ground. He raised his arms upward and began a musical cadence. It was apparent he was singing a song of praise to his victors.

As he sang, Adolf asked Oskar to hand him the Hawkens. He held it above his head and then laid it on the sand in front of him. He was trying to salute the warriors in a manner to suggest understanding. Surprisingly, the old warrior stood up and walked towards Adolf. Immediately, Adolf walked to meet the brave. They stood a couple feet apart and gazed upon each other. The warrior spoke in his language and placed his right hand on his chest as a form of salute.

Then, in broken English, he said, "Kill-From-Afar." He pointed at Adolf. He indicated himself and said, "Spotted Elk." Then he turned and walked away.

Chapter 22

Taking advantage of the temporary truce, the braves quietly gathered their six dead comrades. The braves clearly showed that they were not carrying any weapons, so Adolf, Oskar, and Sven watched in silence. The tingling rush of winning was curtailed. Watching their opposing fighters collect their dead humanized their opponents. A sober silence covered the three like a wool blanket.

After a lengthy, yet quiet, discussion, the three agreed the Indians were indeed Delaware. The belts around their waists and holding their quivers were wide, woven belts. Also, their feathers were colorful and shaped to slant back, but most telling was their hair. Many had shaved their heads except for a center strip standing straight up like the quills of an angry porcupine.

The Delaware[viii] had ridden away with their dead draped over ponies and the two wounded lying on rapidly constructed travois. Still the young friends sat in silence. Oskar was randomly breaking small twigs into smaller twigs. Sven was drawing nothing in the sand. Adolf just sat as if a Greek statue, staring after the Indians that were no longer in sight.

One of the mules expelled a juicy sounding fart that seemed like the signal for all sound to return. There was not only the squeaking of leather and shifting of the mules and horses, but a whole world full of animals and insects performing their daily routines.

"Should we move up this river some more?" Oskar's question was directed to Adolf, their designated leader. The question brought Adolf back to this world. Sven was also watching the leader with his question in the form of a look.

Adolf stood and said, "Yah. We got a few more hours till dusk. No need to waste the whole day."

The western skyline was displaying an egg yolk-like orange sun surrounded by more orange. Sven was searing three inch platter-sized buffalo steaks on flat rocks that were sitting on bright red coals. The second coffee pot was approaching its demise and the three saddlers and an equal number of pack animals were tucked in for the night. Adolf and Oskar watched Sven turn the sizzling portions of meat overflowing with juice. The hot coals flamed to life momentarily as drippings ran off the makeshift grill.

The long awaited, "Come and get it," prompted the hungry travelers to pull belt knives, stab steaks, and flop them onto tin plates. It was not a formal tea party, so manners were ignored. This was just plain old fill-your-face cramming and chewing.

Supper cleanup was done and bed rolls were ready, but the unspoken consensus was to keep each other company. A clear sky invited every star in North America to shine down on the weary adventurers, yet nobody wanted to give in to sleep. Someone had added fresh wood to the campfire and the pot of coffee seemed to refill itself over and over.

No one knew what to say, but they all sensed a need to talk about the Indian fight. It had to be talked out or it would fester in their minds, inviting nightmares. The wolf had come to the door and no one got ate.

Oskar asked, "Why?" Then he looked at the others, "Can't put my thoughts around it. Why did they just charge straight at us?"

Sven hazarded a guess, "No damn experience. Just plain ole ignorance."

Oskar shook his head and stated, "No, that ain't it. That Spotted Elk guy wasn't a tenderfoot. Did yah see the scars on his chest? He dang well has done lots of fighting."

Again a long period of silence before Sven said, "Ufta, I have never seen any shooting like that Adolf. I know I'm a gosh darn good shot, but in Minnesota there ain't room between trees to shoot that far. Saw it with my own eyes or never woulda believed it."

The mood eased up a little when Sven followed with, "Heh, heh. Did you see me get all spooky eyed? I was so flabbergasted I plumb forgot to load the rifles. Hell, I could of got us killed."

Oskar laughed, "I forgot you hadn't seen Adolf at shooting competitions. His daddy won that big Hawkens. He's told to be the best shot in all Ohio. Damn right, but they don't know Adolf here is even better. That's why I suggested he do the shooting."

Sven chuckled, "I wished someone had let me in on it. Hell, I was right upset because I thought I should shoot. Your secret would of made a fool of me if there was time to argue. Now wouldn't that have been a comeuppance?"

Oskar got real serious again and returned to the subject of the braves' charge, "Still doesn't explain why."

"Like I say," Sven suggested, "they have never seen shooting like Adolf's. He pulled our bacon from the fire."

"It still don't explain the Indians stampeding at us, like a blind bear. They must of thought we were untested pilgrims."

Finally Adolf's voice joined in, "Surprised."

Sven looked at Adolf and then over to Oskar as he shrugged his shoulders, "What you mean surprised?"

"Did you notice they all had bows and arrows? Not a gun amongst them," Adolf said thoughtfully. "Them ole boys never seen rifles like ours."

Sven answered, "Huh?"

Adolf continued explaining, "The rifles they are used to fighting are the old flintlocks. Pretty sure they expected to get a lot closer before being fired upon and with less accuracy. Why, I do reckon them braves were a thinking not to lose more than one man before they could weight us down with arrows. They were *surprised*."

Oskar spoke up in a high pitched voice of excitement, "Adolf, you are damned right. That does make a bunch of sense."

Sven thought for a while and in a new tone said, "Ya betcha." Then he shook his big ole head and whispered, "Them poor bastards."

After some more small talk, all the boys drifted to their bedrolls,
Without much wait, they were sound asleep and had no bad dream
amongst them.

Chapter 23

Old man Sun was peeking over the edge in the East to see if they noticed him and saw that all nine travelers were partaking breakfast. Six travelers ate moist green grass and three ate biscuits and jerky. Sven threw a stick at Oskar to get his attention, than pointed his foot long Arkansas toothpick towards Adolf. Adolf was fully engrossed with a huge Siberian Elm. They both squinted at the bark expecting a snake or something to be attached, but there was nothing. "What are you gawking at?" Oskar ventured.

Adolf didn't respond, so Sven tossed a stick at him. When Adolf gave him the evil eye, Sven said, "What the hell are you looking at? Only thing there is that big ole tree."

"Did you ever cut into one of them tree warts?" Adolf asked. "The inside is all swirled around. Damn pretty it is." Then he grinned at his friends, "I was thinking what a tobacco pipe from that wood would look like. I betcha it would be a glorious sight." He tossed the dregs from his cup and stood up. "Sven, where have you got your saw hidden? Let's cut that bump off that elm. I'm going to carve me a pipe."

"Well look at that." Oskar was holding the round chunk of wood and looking and shaking his head. "I have seen many of them there lumps on trees, but I never paid no mind to what they looked like inside. You is right Adolf, them twisted grains are pretty."

Sven said, "Cut lots of building timbers up north, but thought nothing of those deformed things. Ufta, look at all them different colors." He repacked the cross cut; while Adolf placed the bore into his pack. Then Sven looked over to Oskar. They both wandered if Adolf would ever cease to amaze them.

"All this buffalo meat won't keep long," Sven announced, "We need to make jerky."

Adolf nodded his head, "It will take us a couple days to dry, but you're right."

They decided to use all the meat, figuring they could get fresh meat later. They cut it into $1/8^{th}$ inch thick strips of various lengths. Sven found some wild garlic bulbs, ground them up, and added salt. They made drying racks by suspending small limbs balanced between two branched sticks stuck in the ground out in the sun and hung the strips to cure for two days. The meat turned black by the next morning and was dry by the second morning. The dried meat tasted damn good!

They had also decided to finish scraping the buffalo hide and stacked it over a fire of green grass to smoke out the varmints such as ticks, fleas, and lice. The second day, they mashed up the buffalo brain and rubbed it into the scraped hide. The hide was dunked into the river before staking it tightly stretched in the sun to cure. The final step was the slow process of pulling it across a smooth piece of wood to make it pliable.

After the meat was dried and hide processed, they continued on their journey.

"The river looks shallow enough to cross here. Let's cross and follow it on the north side," Adolf suggested. They were pretty sure this was either the Kansas River or the Smoky Hill River. If it was the Kansas, it would separate as both the Smoky Hills and the Republican would come together to form the Kansas. Their plan was to follow the Smoky Hills River.[ix]

The river was one hundred feet across at this spot and shallow with a sandy bottom. Halfway across was a sandbar about twenty feet wide. The group got to the north side with no mishaps. At noon the river became two; one running from the north and one from due east. They rode east and by evening were sitting on another fork in the river, but one fork was flowing from the south. As they studied, they determined the south river was the *Smoky Hill River* and the other the *Saline*; which meant the previous fork was the *Solomon*. As planned, they followed the *Smoky Hill River*.

Still following the river, they made camp and turned in for the night. Adolf thought about suggesting a guard, but decided the horses and mules would be good watch dogs. They did keep their rifles handy just in case. His concern for a guard did cause Adolf to fall asleep with memories of their fight with the Delaware running through his head and prompted bad dreams.

He was taking aim at the lead brave, but when he fired the Hawkens the .54 ball melted before striking. The two Kentucky long rifles had the same effect. Sven and Oskar were screaming at him and pointing at a sky full of arrows.

He awoke to find his shirt was soaked in sweat. He decided to think of something pleasant to divert his mind. Caroline's beautiful face swam into view as he fell back asleep.

Again he was taking aim with the Hawkens, but he didn't fire the rifle. Oskar's and Sven's screams changed to the sound of women yelling. When he looked at his friends, he saw Caroline and Neale waving rolling pins while pleading with him to shoot. He tried to tell them he couldn't find the trigger on his rolling pin, but the Indians were on top of them with their own rolling pins.

This time Adolf flew awake with the Hawkens in his hands and was standing up, looking for the Indians. Yee Gods, this would not do. Adolf stirred the coals to life and added sticks to the fire. The coffee pot was already filled with water and grounds, so he brewed a pot. He took his cup and rifle over to a downed tree, determined to be night watchman.

As he sat there his thoughts drifted back to his parents with his dad repeating over and over – *'It's just a bad dream, Adolf, just a dream.'* For God's sake, he was too old for nightmares – wasn't he?

Chapter 24

They had traveled for more than a week without any more Indian attacks, real or dreamed, before reaching another split in the river - the convergence of the north fork and south fork of the *Smoky Hills River*. Oskar asked Adolf, "Ain't this water about to quit flowing?"

"Yep," answered Adolf, "We're about to reach where it starts. Then we'll jump up to catch the *Republican River* where it heads north, but we will backtrack it east a ways then look for the *South Platt*."

Sven yelled out, "Hey look! Another ground covering of them big shaggies. Why, I betcha there are more of them on these plains than fish in the ocean."

"Seems to be that way, doesn't it?" Oskar responded as they looked out over the backs of buffalo as far as they could see to the south. "Bet they'll be here long after mankind has all killed each other."

"We should cross here and follow the north branch," Adolf suggested, reining his gelding into the narrow water flow. "This is only a couple feet deep. Better fill up on water. No telling when this seepage gives out."

"Hey, can we do some fishing?" Sven was looking into the shallow water as Blue splashed across. "These are brook trout. I'll catch us a bunch for supper." He was the fisherman in the group since he had learned when he was a tadpole in the lake-filled Minnesota country.

"That does sound tasty," Oskar replied, "They are beautiful and plump looking. See how they twinkle in them sun rays?"

After setting the stock to graze, the boys were lounging around on the bank like truant school boys. Oskar and Sven had jerry-rigged some fishing poles and baited them with chunks of jerky. Adolf didn't like fishing, so he was carving on the block of wood he had cut from the elm wart. Somewhere in that chunk of wood he had found the smoking pipe he envisioned, and he was putting the finishing touches on it.

They were swapping lies and looking ahead to gathering up them mustangs. "Think them wild ponies going to be tough to round up?" Oskar asked to no one in particular. "I never have gathered live creatures from nature."

Sven yanked on his pole and walked up the grassy slope, dragging a angry nine inch trout flopping up the bank. "Ufta! Adolf, how many does this make?"

Adolf spoke real soft, "Don't neither of you make any sudden moves. Stay calm and peek across the other side." This was their Adolf advising and they trusted him like their own mommies, so they stayed very still. Then each cast their looks to the south bank.

How can something be so pretty and scary all at once? It was a nice picture-like grouping of five copper-skinned Injun braves astraddle brown and whited splotched pinto ponies. They were all decorated with feathers, both Injuns and ponies. A regal looking warrior with another of them war bonnets streaming black and white eagle feathers was holding a long stick with a crook at the top like a biblical sheep herder, only this was covered with chicken hawk feathers. This was no Delaware brave and he was the only one of the five wearing a shirt. The shirt was made from beautiful, white pronghorn skin, decorated with colorful beads and a porcupine breast shield. His black and white pinto had a red handprint on his rump and a round deerskin shield painted with white and turquoise symbols hanging next to his knee. Unlike all the Indians they had seen, this one was wearing buckskin breeches. It was obvious from both his clothes and his bearing that he was their chief.

The other four were not as decked out, but looked mighty handsome in loin clothes and long black hair in two long pigtail braids. They all had some kind of a round disk attached high on one braid with one to three eagle feathers hanging down, along with strips of rawhide doodads strung with red and white beads. Their bows were wrapped with buckskin and dangled black crow feathers.

These were definitely not like any tribe the three had ever seen. Their faces were not painted and they did not seem aggressive. They were just calm, almost peaceful. Adolf stood up very slowly and held his right hand palm out at shoulder height.

The chief duplicated Adolf's gesture and grunted some words in a soft flowing rhythm that was musical, although not in any language the three understood. After reverting to hand signals, it was apparent they had never seen fishing done in the manner that Oskar and Sven were using. Adolf motioned the Indians to cross over and, understanding his gesture, they rode their ponies splashing through the shallow river.

The chief obviously thought Adolf was also a chief. He leapt off his pinto and walked to Adolf. Putting his hand on his chest and said, *"Mi-hah-min-est."*

Adolf listened closely and repeated it back. The Chief nodded and smiled.

Adolf put his hand on his chest and said. "Nagel."

Mi-hah-min-est concentrated hard and repeated, "Naa- gul," which was close enough for Adolf. Later at Fort Williams the chief's name was translated for them as Spirit Walking and they were told he was one of the main chiefs for the Suhtai clan of the peaceful Cheyenne Nation.

The other four braves joined Oskar and Sven to examine their fishing poles more closely. A couple experimented with the two poles with no success, but all six were laughing and having fun. One brave walked into the river and crouched over. He stood very still and then cupped both hands into the water and scooped out a trout. He continued the motion throwing it to the riverbank to flop around like, well, like a fish out of water.

Oskar joined the Indian in the river and tried his hand at the Indian's method. Sven joined in with the other three bucks to laugh at Oskar's failures. The chief resembled Adolf's solemn appearance but a grin of mirth turned the corners of his mouth upward. He turned to Adolf and gestured at the pipe that Adolf had just finished. Adolf handed it to him and the chief rolled it in his hands and seemed to be admiring it. Adolf reached into his vest pocket to retrieve tobacco and a Lucifer.

The chief understood and handed the pipe back to Adolf to be packed and lit. After Adolf got the pipe lit and blew some smoke, he handed it back to the chief who was anxious to try the pipe. His eyes got round when he tasted the cherry flavored tobacco and he mumbled some form of appreciation. After a couple puffs he started to hand the pipe back, but Adolf smiled and held both hands with palms out and pointed to the chief. The chief looked Adolf in the eye and nodded. He then took out his tomahawk. It consisted of an elk jawbone attached with rawhide to a branch wrapped in pronghorn skin. He gave a long speech that got the attention of his braves before handing it to Adolf. The four warriors yelled out some type of applause, so Oskar and Sven clapped their hands, and then returned to their own fun.

The laughter of the six young men reached a new peak when Oskar slipped and fell into the river, getting both him and his teacher soaking wet. Oskar was laughing the loudest, which pleased the braves. He drove his hand into the river, sending a well-directed steam of water to splash the brave. The water fight was on when the other four joined in.

As they finally exited the water to lie on the bank they were chuckling like boys skinny-dipping in the neighborhood swim hole. It grew quiet as Sven stood to pull his wet shirt over his head. It was obvious that at over six and a half feet tall he was much taller than these lean men of about five foot eight. As though seeing a giant grizzly for the first time, the Indians' eyes grew real round as did their mouths. All of them were well muscled, but none had ever seen slabs of bulging muscles as on this blond, pasty-skinned Swede. Even the chief's expression had changed to one of awe.

Curiosity crept in and the biggest brave challenged Sven to a wrestling match by using one of his buddies to show what he meant. When Sven faced off with the brave, he surprised them by pointing at both braves. The two crouched with arms spread, but Sven just stood there like a black bear. The two circled him looking for an opening. Thinking they saw one, they lunged forward. With the speed of some poisonous rattlesnake, Sven grabbed the arm of one and tossed him about a mile up the bank. The other brave had grabbed Sven's tree trunk legs to throw him to the ground. For a few seconds, Sven seemed to be amused by the brave's lack of success, but then he grabbed the Indian by the waist and lifted him straight up over his head. Sven was holding him like an uncle playing with his baby nephew. The Indian's face was beet red with anger as he squirmed to get loose, arms and legs flailing like a bug on its back. Sven exploded with laughter as did all the others, including Adolf and the chief. The brave heard the laughter, which made him madder, but then he started giggling like the baby toddler he resembled.

After Sven put him down, all of the braves' curiosity overcame any shyness. They all took turns feeling Sven's hard-packed muscles. A couple even ran to their horses to come back carrying decorated sticks to touch Sven to take coup so they could brag to others. The four braves introduced themselves, so Sven and Oskar did likewise. They laughed when Sven identified himself as *Nelson*. Spotted Crow, the brave Sven had held in the air, slapped Sven's chest and stated a name they found out later meant *Yellow Grizzly*. Even the chief laughed and nodded at this new name.

With an overwhelming feeling of accomplishment, the young travelers watched their new friends ride into the tall grass. Out in the middle of the far outback they had experienced a wonder that none had ever contemplated. They felt at peace with this wonderful prairie land and all its glories.

Chapter 25

It was on day 32 that they first glimpsed the distant Rocky Mountains. The mountains were hazy and distorted by heat waves, but they could see a purple mass with snowcapped peaks set against the clear blue sky.

A few days back, they had come to the headwaters of the Republican River and were now following the South Platt River. It had taken them almost two days to reach the South Platt after leaving the Republican, two days over nothingness; just wide open space of grass under the awesome heavens of this land. The grass was a shorter version of the same prairie grass that had tickled their horses' bellies earlier in the journey. Buffalo and antelope were both in abundance, and were joined by jackrabbits the size of small deer. The boys agreed that the long eared, big-footed bunnies were of a size large enough to be predators rather than prey.

Several times they had seen Indians similar to the five friends they had met on the Smoky Hills River. The mule skinners they talked to in Missouri had told them that the tribes closer to the mountains were Cheyenne and Arapaho – both considered nonaggressive. Many of the Indians they saw verified this claim by waving. Some were small groups of hunters, but most were traveling tribes that included old white-haired warriors, women, children and dogs that followed the migrating buffalo.

Glancing ahead, Adolf interrupted Oskar's background chatter, "Guess we'll be at the foot of those tall hills late tomorrow. Do you want to traipse up to that new Fort Williams? The wild mustangs should be straight west of there." While waiting for a response, he halted Buck to adjust his cinch and give him a bucket of water.

Sven dropped off his grulla and tried to stretch the kinks out of his back. He took the time to adjust Blue's gear and give him water before responding. He looked to the north, "Reckon that fort is open for business?"

"That's what I heard."

Oskar put his derby back on after watering his mare and mule. He chimed in, "Hope they have beer. I have a deep thirst for the taste of beer, even warm."

Their spirits were lightened, because they knew trip's end was close. They all climbed back into the saddle and started off at a fast walk. The mountains filled in with detail the closer they got.

At dawn the next day, they were wide awake with expectation. They breakfasted on lard-fried potatoes with strips of buffalo jerky. They downed their coffee. Afterward, they washed pans and utensils in the river, using sand to scrub the grease off and drying them with handfuls of grass. As they saddled the horses and packed the mules, Oskar looked at the Rockies, "I reckon them is the most mountains I ever seen. Why they near to poking a hole in that blue sky."

Being his normal conversationalist self, Adolf nodded his head. Sven said, "Ya betcha."

By noon they were at the base of the foothills. These big peaks were not only bigger than what they were used to, they were plain different looking. The poplar and lesser trees gave way to quaking aspen, blue spruce, fir, and gigantic ponderosa pine. Some were twisted by the wind like a baby giant had thrown a tantrum. But the most notable difference was ridges of huge bare rock in many colors. Sven took his hat off and used his kerchief to wipe his forehead, "Them are just plain beautiful, yet wild as a newborn mountain lion. Surely must be God's temple. Ufta, I admit, I am downright awestruck."

Oskar was so tongue-tied, he actually said nothing. Adolf responded with his usual nod.

They lunched on elk jerky and yesterday's cold flatbread, which was washed down with clear mountain runoff from nearby bubbling streams.

What a contrast! There was wide-open prairie on their right and a wall of towering mountains on their left. Adolf felt they were traveling on the edge between two different worlds. Hearing a rumble, the travelers looked to the northwest where dark gray clouds were climbing over the mountaintops. Their menacing intent was announced by bolts of crackling lightening. The young men pulled their slickers from behind their saddles to slide into, but the cool rain was already upon them. By the time the gray slickers were buttoned up it was time to take them back off, because the sudden thunderstorm was off to the east over the prairie and a clear blue sky was peering down on them.

Oskar started in giggling as he said, "Wasn't that a danged queer deal? Done soaked but my slicker didn't hardly get wet."

Both Sven and Adolf burst out laughing. Adolf responded, "Don't seem to need slickers out here." Even though wet, they were comfortable in the dry heat of this new territory. They all knew their damp clothes would be dry in a few miles with the constantly blowing warm wind.

All three men were very much in the present, absorbing the splendor put on their table by mama nature, but the majority of their thoughts were focused on their future, everything unknown. Yet, none were worried or concerned. They were not even committing to a well laid-out plan, only to an idea, an unfounded idea at that. Oskar and Sven trusted Adolf's ingenuity, but both knew Adolf's dream was only a hunch; it was not based on facts or knowledge. If they were experienced businessmen, they would not be on this quest that was similar to Don Quixote's impossible dream.

The list of unknowns was longer than any wide-eyed nine year old's list to Santa. Would they find mustangs? Could they capture them? Could they train them? Was there a market to sell them? Could they develop a new breed of working ponies? Was there a future need for them? It wasn't that they were sure of success, as much as failure didn't matter. It wasn't knowledge that was needed. It was luck and knowing they would do their best. All three were only eighteen and could start over. A one in a hundred chance was at least a chance. If they found a way to make it happen then they would be men of vision.

Adolf pointed to a fast flowing river that was tumbling out of the mountains. The three discussed the opening in the Rockies and decided to take a look, since they were only two days or less from Fort William.[x]

They had only traveled about five miles when the valley expanded into a beautiful meadow with the river cutting through. The meadow was a mile long and a mile or two wide, filled with beautiful green grass. It was hard to determine the width, because it was so irregular shaped. On the south side of the meadow were jagged rock formations jutting in and a couple of box canyons extending into the tall trees, each with spring-fed lakes. It was made even more beautiful by several acres of white barked quaking aspen trees with their namesake leaves shimmering in the breeze.

North of the river was a fifty foot high wall of solid rock topped with evergreen trees extending straight up into the heavens above. A couple of white-headed eagles were showing off their flying skills. The rocks were not rounded - they were jagged flat chunks of rock resembling the grain in a split firewood log. Here they were mostly white with streaks of black, but higher up they were many colors. Even the river was filled with rocks, causing the water to splash and change direction; bouncing along like a teenager late for supper. Clear water was marred by the white splashes along with flashes of the reflected sun rays. Adolf wanted to stare forever into the river at the dazzling display of multi-colored smooth stones on the river bottom.

Oskar laughed, "I see why these are called the Rocky Mountains." He pointed at the jagged rocks, "Seems Odin's been here with his big ole hammer."

Adolf cast aside his normal stoic bearing as excitement bubbled through him. "My God, this is it! This is beyond all my fanciful dreams. I want this spot to be our ranch, our future."

Oskar joined his boyhood friend and, without any show of restraint, wrapped his arm around Adolf's shoulders. "It is like a dream coming to life. This is as good as it gets. I wonder if there are more valleys beyond."

Their big friend squatted on his heels beside them. As if they could all see the same dream, he softly proclaimed, "Ufta, just a big ole ufta. This is just like what I done seen when Adolf spoken to us. You betcha, this is worth the ride." He jumped up and hugged his friends, "Let's ride a little yonder and see if God has tapped us on the shoulder with a good luck stick."

They hobbled the mules to a nearby yearling jack pine and trotted their long-legged ponies through God's creation. They came to a small waterfall and galloped up the rise in elevation beside it. They emerged into a hanging valley about twice the size of the first, but no less beautiful.

"Why there is enough elbow room for us to all raise large families!" Oskar took his hat off to run his hand through his bushy red hair, "Course, first I need to scout out a willing filly that will have me." He slapped Sven across his broad shoulders with his dusty hat then crumpled to the ground in joyful laughter.

Sven reached a massive hand to tickle Oskar's tummy, saying, "What honey would ever hook up with a red spotted poon dog like you?"

Adolf was already thinking ahead of the game, "When we get to Fort William, we'll ask if a squatter's claim will make this ours. There sure ain't anybody else out here to dispute our claim, but someday they will come. They'll come in swarms like bees to clover blossoms." He swung off his gray dun and motioned for his friends to join him as he knelt on one knee. The three took hold of hands, forming a circle, and Adolf sent a prayer of thanks to the Father above.

Chapter 26

Fort William sure didn't look like what they expected for a wilderness fort. There was a fort, but it was made from thick adobe instead of timber. A good sized firing station was built above the gate. The American flag was dancing a merry jig overhead, but surrounding the fort were animal skin teepees and Indian families carrying on normal lives. There were several dogs barking at every movement and brown and white or black and white pinto and paint ponies tied everywhere. Indian children played some game with a ball and sticks. It looked more like an Indian powwow than a military defense of the West, but it sure enough was the new Fort William.

Nobody gave them any mind as they rode through the Indian encampment and into the fort. Blue coated soldiers were everywhere - on the ramparts, over by the barracks and marching to some loud-mouthed, wooly faced brute with three yellow inverted V's on his sleeves.

Loud laughter from a tent surrounded by grimy men in filthy buckskins strongly suggested where the beer was being served. As they pulled up to a tie rail, a blue blast of swear words burnt their ears. The source was a man tugging who was an Arkansas toothpick out of his shin, letting blood flow into his filthy moccasins. "Jeb, you bastard, you stuck me on purpose," accused the man. His partner in their game of mumblety peg was standing with his feet widespread, but was giggling so hard his eyes were watering. Both men were so drunk that neither could stand, much less see where they were throwing the knife. But the bleeding man snorted and threw the knife at the ground, impaling his friend's left foot, which brought out howls of laughter from both.

Shaking his head in disgust, Adolf advised, "You two get us a table and some beers. I'm going to find the head man."

Sven jumped off his grulla and took the reins for the mule Adolf was leading. He tied it to the rail along with his mule and horse. Oskar tied Patches and his mule to the same rail and responded to Adolf's advice, "Better hurry back if you want any beer. I'm dry as a desert and we all seen Sven drink up." He chuckled at his own joke as he slapped his knee and pushed Sven into the noisy tent.

Adolf stopped beside a soldier shoveling manure and asked, "Where can I find the head honcho around this ole fort?"

The shirtless man asked back, "You all mean the commander?" When Adolf nodded, he continued, "That's Major Hitchcock. He would be in the tent over there where the guard is standing."

Adolf touched his brim with two fingers and received a smiling salute from the horse-poop collector. Smiling to himself, Adolf rode Buck to the indicated tent. When he walked to the tent, the guard snapped his feet together and raised his rifle in front of him, bellowing, "Halt. What's your business?"

Adolf stated, "I'm here to talk to the major."

"Sergeant Major, a civilian wants to chat with the commander."

A large, dark haired man with all kinds of yellow stripes on his sleeves came to the tent opening and glared at Adolf. He had a walrus-like mustache that joined up with bushy, mutton chop sideburns. He was so starched looking that Adolf wondered if he ever sat down or just leaned in a corner.

"I'm Sergeant Major O'Malley," he extended his hand in a cordial manner.

Adolf introduced himself and said he would like to ask the major some questions. The Irishman told Adolf to wait a minute and went back inside.

A few minutes later, a man in his early thirties walked out and extended his hand. His blue coat came to mid-thigh and a gold colored leaf was on each shoulder. His lip hair drooped down below his chin and was heavily waxed and twisted upward at the ends. He introduced himself as Major Hitchcock.

Adolf sat in front of the major's desk on a rickety, folding camp chair; which felt like it was going to break apart or collapse with the slightest movement. The major led Adolf through the niceties, including having the Sergeant Major bring coffee. He corrected Adolf's us of Fort William and explained the replacement fort had been named Fort John after one of the American Fur Company partners, a John Sarpy; then the major asked what he could do for Adolf.

Adolf outlined his want-to-dos. When he told the officer about catching mustangs, Major Hitchcock interrupted him, "Are you planning on selling any of these ponies?"

"If we could find a buyer, selling some would provide us some seed money."

"We might be able to help each other out. The army is always in need of mounts. I could pay you $15 a head for green broke ponies. I need several here, but I damn well know the other outposts need all they can get their hands on."

Adolf didn't hesitate, just stuck his hand out and said, "Deal."

The young officer opened a desk drawer and brought out a fifth of bourbon and two mismatched glasses. "Let's have a toast on this." He poured two fingers in each glass and handed one to Adolf as he said, "To a beneficial partnership." He tapped Adolf's glass with his and drank the entire drink in one swallow. Adolf did the same and tried to keep from coughing as the burning liquor left a trail of ashes all down to his belly.

The major questioned Adolf, "Was there anything else you wanted to talk about?"

"I do have some questions you might be able to answer for me."

Adolf told him about the land they had found south of the fort. Major Hitchcock motioned for Adolf to join him at a huge map covering the back wall of the tent. Adolf was able to point at the river where the valleys were located.

The major told Adolf that valley was in the Kansas Territory, "That river was newly named a few years back with the French name Cache La Poudre River. It has something to do with some fur trappers, if I remember right.

"There is no settlement going on in that area, but no reason you couldn't squat there. Someday the government will open all these territories for settlers coming west. Right now that is in the Ute or Pawnee hunting grounds, both are easily agitated."

"Would they attack us?"

"Damn tooting they would. They're darn right ornery in that way and we can't protect you on that land. It is marked as Indian Territory. But I can't order you not to settle there. If you want, I can make a record of your claim so when homesteaders come, and they will, you have first right to file. I will make a note to let you know if that land is opened for homesteaders."

"Thank you kindly, sir."

"Where are you planning to look for these Mustangs?"

Adolf squinted his eyes and answered, "Heard there may be some herds west of here. Are you aware of where they might be found?"

"Yah, there are several large herds about forty to sixty miles west - all you will ever need." Major Hitchcock grew a huge grin on his face as he said, "I believe I can provide you good news. If you are planning on being on the Cache you might want to just follow it west to the Sand

Creek River. You'll find a few thousand of the wild mustangs right there."

Adolf couldn't believe his luck, "How far across there are they?"

"I would guess less than forty miles, but there are more herds south of there also. " The Major started laughing, "You will be on land that the Utes think is their hunting ground." He walked over to the map and drew his finger from the foothills to a basin further west. "The Utes are kind of different. Their tribes are basically extended families, but they get together to hunt or fight. They are very protective of their lands, so keep your eyes open."

They shook hands after some more discussion, and Adolf headed to the beer tent to pass on the good news to his partners. He found Oskar and Sven slamming down beers and hooting up a storm.

A bull-legged, lean man in his late twenties approached the three with four beer mugs, "Howdy, you all. Are you all going to chase them wild mustangs further west? If you all say yes, I brought over some suds and I want to chat you up."

Now the boys were not so impolite as to turn away free drinks, so before long it was four rowdy men trying to out boast each other. Each one was exaggerating each story beyond human belief. Their new friend was Cokey Bernard from West Texas, who claimed to be a 'durn good' wrangler. Cokey said, "Why, I can rope a tornado and clinch it down to a dust devil. I can stick on any bucking horse like a tick on a dog." As he whipped the foam hitching a ride on his bushy lip hair, he grinned and said, "I been shooting guns since momma took away my last diaper. I can shoot a fly off a buffalo's pooper without nicking a hair."

Even chatty Oskar seemed quiet beside this braggart. But they had taken a liking to this older gent and were damn pleased when he asked if he could join them catching mustangs. If half his brags were close to fact, he had skills they needed. He had gone into Nevada territory twice to catch wild mustang ponies to break and sell to Texas ranchers. He had heard there were some in the Wyoming territory and came up to see for himself.

They accepted his assistance and shared another beer to seal the agreement.

Adolf then told his buddies what Major Hitchcock mentioned about the herds west of the land they found on the Cache la Poudre River. He also filled them in on the major's offer to buy horses for the army at $15 a head and about claiming the valley land. They got frisky with that news and the discussion at the table became excited and loud.

"I hear tell you tenderfeet aim to squat side the Cache." The four all turned their heads towards the gravelly voice spraying from the white haired trapper. At least, they surmised he was a trapper; his stink was worse than an overflowing outhouse. He was wearing buckskins head to toe, but they had no hazard as to the origin of the skins. Grimy was too tame a word for these filthy, flea-infested wrappings. The skins had probably seen better days, but that had to have been several years ago. Black blotches of dried blood, dried up chunks of animal guts, and various colors of dirt decorated the skins like a collage.

Even more noticeable were the number of guns and knives tucked everywhere. Even a well-polished Hawkens rifle was clutched in his scarred right hand, in contrast to the six or seven flintlock pistols and up-teen knives loading him down. Two vicious looking tomahawks were jammed in his beaded belt.

Without asking, he grabbed a chair and hunkered down at their table. "Most call me Caribou Sam, at lessen they do if they don't want to get cut some. I don't rightly remember my family name, heh, heh. I's been in the tall and lonesome since them trees were knee high. I traps, that's what I does. I's kilt twenty griz'es." With this, he pulled out several necklaces made from bear claws that were hanging on his chest.

Holding his breath, Adolf introduced everybody and offered to buy the old timer a beer.

"I thankee friend. Damn right neighborly. I say thankee," grinned Sam. "Let me tell the facts. Some of the Frenchies had it to mind to scatter out of them rocks, running from a big snow in. They planted their extra kegs of powder in the river banks. Cache la Poudre is Frenchie words for 'hide the powder'. And that is the blame truth."

He chugged his beer and set the mug on the table. Caribou Sam stood up on wobbly legs and said, "Gud luck," then he wandered off to find another benefactor.

Chapter 27

The group of four finished their beer and gathered at the trading store just outside the fort to replenish their dwindling supplies. They didn't know how long they would be out in the valley, so they filled up their larders – thirty pounds of coffee, hundred pounds of flour, fifty pounds of sugar, thirty pounds of salt, hundred pounds of pinto beans, and, at Cokey's suggestion, three hundred feet of hemp rope. They also loaded up on powder, bars of lead and caps, along with the molds to make their own lead balls. Also purchased were four more double-headed axes and a couple of two-handled cross cut saws. At the last minute, they decided to buy a twenty foot square of oiled canvas and a large, mildewed army surplus tent. They asked the clerk about a wagon and were told he had two out back he used to haul furs, but was willing to sell one.

After looking the wagons over, Sven picked the one that he said was in better shape than the other. He even haggled with the clerk, pointing out flaws and got the price down several dollars. Adolf rolled off some paper bills from their dwindling stash to pay for everything.

Out front, they unloaded the three mules and Cokey's mustang pack horse. As they redistributed the loads to the wagon, a gathering crowd of gawking trappers and soldiers gathered. The crowd was all too happy to shout out instructions for packing, along with snide remarks about various articles. The travelers hooked two of the draft mules to the wagon and tied Sven's blue dun and Cokey's mustang pack horse to the back of the wagon.

Along with the yellow pack horse, Cokey had two saddler buckskin mustangs. Adolf, Oskar and Sven were a little concerned about how small they were compared to their long-legged Trotters. Oskar voiced their concern and their new friend started laughing out loud. Then he said, "You fools have never seen these horses move, have you?" Chuckling, he jumped on one of his mounts and put the little pony through his paces. First, he took off in a cloud of dust and stopped him on a dime, leaving nine cents in change. Cokey casually held the reins in one hand and let the horse go to work cutting one mule from the other animals. Each time the irritated mule tried to change directions, the lightning-fast steed was in front of it. It was like a dance step without music.

Even the crowd was awed. Sounds of "See that?", "My Gawd" , and "Wow' floated through the air. Cokey dismounted with a bow, to cheers and clapping. The mule, pissed off, dashed over to stand by the wagon.

Cokey's three new friends were standing there in shock. Oskar was first to break the silence, "Now that was downright pretty."

"That is a cutting pony in action," Cokey said with a smile, "And that's why cowboys wants 'em real bad."

Adolf spoke up, "Pards, we are headed to a successful future. This will work."

Having sufficiently impressed them, Cokey showed the other three his campsite outside the fort. It was large enough for all of them for the night. Sven grabbed some dry grass and sticks to start a fire while the others rounded up fire wood for the night. After eating steaks and the last of their potatoes, the trading post didn't have any to buy, they sat around slurping black java and trading whoppers.

The next morning Cokey made them some pancakes and bacon along with their morning strong, get-the-eyes-open coffee. Then they prepared to start their journey back to the Cache la Poudre River. The first few miles were quiet, with four minds daydreaming of this great adventure. But, before long, Oskar started his normal chatting and then Cokey joined right in with his own babble. Sven and Adolf shook their heads and accepted that from now on their travels were going to be twice as loud.

Adolf rode Buck south along the east side of the foothills, thinking that he was actually very comfortable with the jaybird duet behind him. The competing chatter reminded him he was very lucky. He was with friends on a very exciting adventure that promised to provide them all a lifetime of happiness. Caroline would join him in this new land to create life beyond all expectations. He was confident they were trailblazers, not dissimilar to the pioneers who risked everything to sail across the ocean to the unknown continent of North America. *'Life is what you make of it,'* his dad used to preach to him and his brothers. He was driven by something he could not explain, but he knew it was his destiny to start a life in this untamed land in the Kansas Territory. It actually felt like he was being pulled toward some form of greatness.

His mind drifted to each member of his cast of explorers. Each was unique and it seemed God had selected them to be with him for a reason.

Oskar was his oldest friend and was as loyal as a mother bird to her chicks. He chatted to no end, but even that was comforting. He understood Adolf's need to be quiet and respected it. His chatter was not a distraction, but a reminder that Adolf was not alone. Oskar understood Adolf better than any other person on this earth, including his parents. Oskar would follow him without question; he had Adolf's back. He was also fantastic with horses. He was sensitive and knew how to get their affection, plus believed the same as Adolf that gentleness was the key for training horses, not cruelty. Horses did better if they wanted to please you than if they were afraid of you.

Sven was totally different than Oskar, but also had a gentle nature. Even though he had the size and strength to force his will, that was not his nature. Sven's muscle would come in handy, but was not something to fear. Additionally, he had skills for building and making things. Although they had never discussed it, they all knew that Sven could build whatever they would need for their ranch. Plus he had a great capacity to learn and was not restricted by any need to be right.

Cokey was new and a chatterbox himself, but he was not trying to interrupt Adolf's thoughts by getting him into a conversation. He seemed to understand and respect Adolf's quiet nature as well as Oskar did. Cokey's knowledge of the ponies was needed and his skills for training the mustangs complemented the rest of them in their lack of these needs. Adolf did not believe it was pure luck that Cokey had found them; that was a higher power at work. It was like God said '*your team is weak in one area, so this man is who you need*'.

On reflection, Adolf knew that these three young men would follow him without question and the four together made one powerful team. His dream was there to achieve and it would happen. The hardest part was being patient enough to not rush what had to be done. If they built the foundation, the rest would come.

Chapter 28

They crossed the river at a wide spot which slowed down the stampede of the Cache la Poudre. It was shallow enough to wade through. They followed the flow of the river through the foothills to where it was galloping out of the mountains. Adolf, Oskar and Sven stopped at the mouth of the valley to verify that their memories had not been blown out of proportion. Somehow, it was more beautiful on the second viewing. The other's renewed memories were substantiated by Cokey, "Good Golly! I thought you guys were playing me as gullible. I've never seen the like."

The river wasn't wide, only about forty feet, but it was hemmed in by rock wall riverbanks. They could not fathom how many centuries it had taken water to chisel through the rocks. It was not just the deep cut demarking the edges of the river; boulders of all sizes spilled everywhere. The runaway river was banging head-on into boulders sticking out of the water, causing water to spray upwards by several feet in a spectacular water show. The spray sparkled where rays of the sun were reflected. Smarter water was darting around the rocks in a display of white water rapids that offset the sparkling green-blue current. Smaller rocks under the surface caused the water to roll over them in a constant, lifelike heartbeat. The sun in the western sky was throwing beams of sunrays through the water spray, resulting in thousands of tiny rainbows dancing across the surface.

On the north side of the river, a black-streaked white wall of stone rose thirty feet straight up like a manmade dike. On top of that wall was a collage of deciduous and evergreen trees, interrupted in some unknown pattern by rock uprisings in various colors of orange, rust, brown, and purple. On one of the large cliffs higher up, three mountain goats were curiously watching the men.

As remembered, the land south of the river was a huge meadow of two foot high grass. The meadow was showing off its dance steps in rhythm with the gentle breeze passing through the gap on the west end. At the southwest corner stood a couple acres of quaking aspen with slender white trunks demonstrating their namesake as the breeze fluttered the leaves back and forth to display the lighter colored bottom side in contrast with the darker top side. A peninsula of rock wandered in to surround a good-sized shimmering lake. A couple of canyons darted south with sunlight reflecting off the surface of a couple more lakes – plenty of water for livestock.

A gradual incline rose on the south for about forty feet before steepening to a ridiculous upward angle covered with tall green ponderosa pines and shorter blue spruce. Between the meadow and the trees, where the grass was sparser, were hundreds of variations of wildflower – yellow, white, blue, violet and dots of red Indian paint brush.

The river was about five feet below the rock sides, but there were signs that the river was not trained to stay within its boundaries. Washouts were evident where the grass had been washed away and replaced by broken trees and other debris from the mountains above. Most of the water came from melting spring snow.

Displays of tall, snowcapped mountains looked down on their mountain range as if they were reminding them that theirs were just a small piece of this Rocky Mountain world.

The awed travelers decided to set up camp in the meadow on a spot where they could watch the two entrances, in case of Indians. They found a bubbling spring in a rock basin close to the south edge they could use for water. They were close enough to the three visible lakes to provide water and grass for their expected herd of mustangs. The grass was developing seed heads that was added fuel for the animals.

Sven and Adolf hauled out the military tent and laid it on the ground. Oskar and Sven cut four aspen saplings to use for corner tent poles and one taller one for their center pole. This would be their temporary dwelling until they started building structures. When the tent was up, they moved their gear in and selected sleeping places at the back to leave the front for a common area.

Adolf and Cokey collected rocks which they placed in a ten foot circle. They removed the grass from within the circle before digging a two foot deep fire pit. The dirt was packed inside of the rocks to keep fire from getting to the grass. They also removed all the grass within four feet of their fire pit. They did not want to set this valley on fire. Five flat rocks were placed in the pit to use to heat up cooking pots and pans. Two coffeepots were filled with water from the spring and sat on top of two of the flat rocks in the fire pit.

Sven twisted tufts of some of the dryer grass and piled them in the pit along with gathered sticks as kindling, and started a fire. Adolf and Cokey gathered firewood from the abundance of dead limbs lying about. Oskar cut another pole to place in the Y of two trees to hang their meat so animals couldn't reach it. Once the work was done and the antelope steaks were cooking, they sat around the fire and chatted about plans for the next day.

Adolf cupped both hands around his tin cup, "I would like to ride up river and see if we can find them mustangs." As the others nodded, he suggested, "I think we should all stay together for safety."

Cokey scratched the stubble on his chin and asked, "Do you know the tribe claiming this land as their hunting grounds?"

"Major Hitchcock said this is Ute territory." Adolf slid his hands into his gun belt and continued, "They separate their tribes by extended families, but the braves all join together to hunt or fight." With a serious look on his face, he cautioned, "He said they can be real aggressive."

"Yah, we better stay together than. No use getting caught alone and losing our scalps." Oskar leaned to one side to itch his backside, "I do admit them Injuns make me fretful for my hide."

"You're plenty quiet, Mr. Sven. Something got your panties pinching?" Cokey grinned at Sven to ensure the big guy knew it was a joke.

Oskar looked at their friend with some concern, but Adolf just glanced with a knowing look on his face, "Are you thinking of Neale?"

Their blond friend's massive shoulders were hunched over and the brown liquid was about to spill from his forgotten cup. He had a faraway look on his face as if he was mesmerized by the fire, "I damn do miss that lady. I have never felt like this before. I do enjoy you guys' company and I want to find them mustangs, but golly I do like that lady. Know what I mean?"

"Sure do. I have to keep pushing Caroline out of my thoughts or I about weep water from my eyes like a baby separated from its mommy. I just keep telling myself to think of when we have this put together and they are with us."

It got mighty quiet around the campfire. Even the pair of men who didn't have women waiting for them seemed to understand their two friends' feelings. The four were out in the wilderness with the closest people being in Fort John, unless some aggressive Utes were closer. They were on their own. There was no one to come save them if they got in trouble.

"I think those slabs of meat are sizzled to perfection. Let's eat them before they burn," Oskar stated. He stood and jammed his knife into a huge steak, sliding it onto his tin plate. He sliced the steak into oversized bite sized chunks and used his knife to spear one into his mouth. With juices flowing down his chin, he announced, "Tasty, real tasty."

Chapter 29

Oskar opened his eyes to the soft snoring of his friends, two of his friends. He panicked a little, realizing that Adolf was not in the mildew smelling tent. He remembered they had spent the first night in their new valley on the Cache la Poudre River and were in the land of the fierce Ute. He grabbed his Colt and crawled to the tent opening to look out. Nothing! He slithered out of the tent with his thumb on the hammer, ready to cock the pistol as he looked around.

He relaxed when he spied Adolf standing by the white aspen trees, gazing all around the valley. As he watched his boyhood friend, a feeling of tenderness cloaked him. He felt closer to this young man than anyone in the world and it had been that way since they were both six - the first day of school.

Six-year old Oskar was near to pissing his pants as he sat in front of two older boys who were describing in great detail what they intended to do to him during recess. All heads turned to the door as another six year old entered. He stopped and let his eyes survey the one room school house. In spite of his size and age, he radiated confidence, not fear, as his steel gray eyes took in his surroundings. It was like he memorized and judged each person in the room as his eyes slowly moved from person to person. Those knowing eyes stopped and came back to look at Oskar and the two bullies leaning over him. He walked over and sat beside Oskar, simply saying, "Adolf."

Oskar replied, "Hi. I'm Oskar and this is my first day at school ever. What about you?"

Adolf smiled and said, "Yep." He turned his head to the two bullies who were saying they now had two mommy's boys to torture, he simply said, "Get." There was strength in his eyes that the older boys saw and feared. They quickly moved to another desk without saying a word.

That is how Adolf's and Oskar's friendship had been ever since. When he was with Adolf, he felt like there was nothing that could harm them.

"What you doing out here?" Oskar asked as he walked over to his friend and sat on the grass beside him.

Adolf smiled at Oskar and placed a hand on his shoulder, "Look around and tell me what you see."

Oskar knew he was going to fail this test, but he trusted Adolf and looked around the valley. "I see a valley of beautiful green grass between awesome rocky mountains ridges covered with magnificent trees. I see a fast running river under a blue sky. I see thousands of birds and five deer grazing. I see a badger attacking an ant pile and a porcupine and two young ones waddling towards that spring yonder." He smiled at Adolf, very pleased with his own observations, knowing it had been rather complete, "What do you see?"

Adolf grasped his friend's shoulder and gazed across the valley before saying, "I see a log ranch house nestled in front of the aspens. I see a large barn north of the house to block the winter winds and snow. I see a windmill turning in the wind and filling a tank with water. I see a blacksmith shop just south of the house and corrals between the barn and the house. I see a gate next to the river at the east opening. I see a bunkhouse next to the windmill and I see grazing mustangs scattered all around the valley. I see our friends training horses and our wives hanging the wash. Scattered in front of the house and barn I see little children playing. I see our future."

Oskar closed his eyes as Adolf talked and he saw everything Adolf mentioned. He looked at his friend and thanked God for allowing him to be part of his friend's dreams. He nodded his head, "That is damn beautiful." Then he quietly stayed sitting by his partner as they shared a moment of bliss.

They were interrupted by Sven saying, "Hey you two lovey doves, coffee's ready." Their big friend had a puzzled look on his face as he tried to figure out what Adolf and Oskar were doing just sitting there, close together. It wasn't like either to be wasting time. He just shook his head and announced, "Cokey has breakfast burning. Thought we were getting an early start to them wild mustangs? Come on pards, sunlight is burning. Do you hear?"

After their tummies were filled up, Adolf suggested they only take their riding stock and hobble the rest close to a spring. They saddled their rides and, after a second inspection of their camp, they headed to the west gap.

Cokey was flabbergasted when they rode into the bigger meadow, "Well golly, gee. There's more." This valley was at least twice the size of the one they were camped, but it looked wilder. Maybe it was because of all the drift wood and torn turf piled in the flood plain.

As they rode, Adolf announced, "We'll place a gate on the west end of this valley and the east end of the first one. That should keep the horses from wandering. What you think?"

He had to look at his friends to see they were all nodding as if they expected him to hear the nods. He grinned, took his hat off and shook his head.

The river meandered all over the place, but by night fall they had reached a large plateau. Groves of trees were scattered all over as well as sage brush, soap weed, yucca, pear cactus, and all kinds of wildflowers. The plateau had various sized hills, ravines, small catch ponds, and sandy blowouts. It was completely different than the range along the river. Making it more spectacular were thousands of mustangs roaming all over. They were divided into groupings. Some were large herds of fifty or so; mares, colts, and yearlings were watched over by one single majestic stallion for each herd. Smaller herds with younger stallions as their patriarch were visible as well as even younger stallions grouped together in their separate bachelor-only herds.

The mustang's colors were all over the board: red roans, brown bays, tan buckskins, and grays ranging from almost white to a darker blue. Most were duns, depicted by black manes and tails and darker faces and forelegs, with a dark streak on the ridge of their backs. Most stood less than fourteen hands high, except for the stallions which were over fifteen hands. Magnificent muscles proudly displayed scars from the many battles to protect their herds from horny young upstarts.

The four men made camp and fixed their vittles. They sat around their campfire and planned for the next couple of days, before slipping off into individual dreams of the coming roundup.

Chapter 30

The four sweaty and dust covered men took a lunch break of jerky and cold biscuits. The dry fare was washed down with cold water from the spring beside their camp. They were pleased with the day's work – building a catch-pen. They had used dry wood, brush and rocks to create a funnel. At the opening it was about fifty yards wide and it narrowed down to about ten yards, leading into an acre-sized corral. They had dug holes to place ten foot tall poles as deep as they could; which was not very deep because of all the rocks under the surface. To strengthen the shallowly placed poles they had used water, clay and grass to make a mixture of adobe. After the poles were in place and tamped firmly, the adobe and rocks had been poured in each hole. Each pole had a second pole tied with wet rawhide strings near the top that was angled down to the ground on the outside of the corral, forming a triangle with the tips buried into the ground. They were confident that these poles could withstand the beating of panicked mares banging into them. The poles were ten to twelve inches in diameter and made from green, hardwood trees that would not break easily.

After their lunch break, they cut rails to tie between the poles, again using wet rawhide strips as ties. The rawhide would shrink in the sun and tighten onto the wood. By nightfall it was completed and the men were exhausted. For the gate, they had cut four twelve foot timbers to slide across the opening and tied them with hemp rope. They needed to let the rawhide and adobe dry and then test the structure with a collection of horses. But at this moment, they needed to sleep – so they did.

The second day they rose earlier than the birds. It was a peaceful dawn with few sounds. Even the hated mosquitos were still comfortable in their tiny beds. A lone cottontail joined them, as if to ask what they were doing disturbing its sleep. Birds, embarrassed by having people rise before they did, started chirping loudly to remind them who was supposed to wake up first. After private visits to the tall weeds followed by a cold breakfast, they drowsily rode out to scout the closest mustangs and put together their roundup plan.

They watched the various herds rely on some unknown pecking order to visit the various water sites for a morning quenching drink. The next group patiently waited their turn and then replaced the one in front of them; while another herd would replace them in waiting. Always the herd's stallion watched over them all until they were done drinking before walking forward to take his fill. The only disturbance was when a group or rowdy bachelors with too much male hormones and not enough brains tried to impress a group of lady horses. It only took one charge of the palomino stud to flash his teeth and hooves for the younger stallions to turn tail and leave the champion's harem.

"I suggest that tomorrow we wait for one of the large groups to drink up," Adolf was sitting with his back straight as he started talking. "You notice how the stallions always leave last? We will wait close to our pen and split the herd."

The others nodded their heads, Adolf continued, "We will drive half into our pen and let the other half escape. The stallion will have to choose which group to follow, so we will encourage him to follow those escaping."

161

Oskar spoke up first and confirmed he liked the plan.

Cokey was next to speak up, "You all mean we won't even have to lasso them? That's sneaky. Is that even fair?"

Oskar and Sven slapped him on the head with their hats as they chuckled. Cokey fell down in a heap and tried to roll away laughing, "Yah all gonna make me piss my pants. Leave me be."

The three rowdy wranglers quit their horsing around and hurried to catch up with Adolf, who was riding toward their campsite. By the time they caught up, Adolf was gathering tinder to start a noon fire. They wrapped their reins around a rail of the corral beside Buck and pitched in preparing a warm meal of stew. The stew consisted of venison chunks, along with wild turnips, wild carrots, and wild onions. After cleaning their utensils, they split up to ride around their catch-pen and check how the adobe and rawhide was drying. They pushed against the rails and were satisfied that they would hold the wild mustangs slamming against them; although when Sven pushed against some they all held their breath.

Oskar rode off to hunt and came back about an hour later with a young doe across Patches' hindquarters and a couple of prairie hens hanging from his saddle. Sven grabbed the doe and started skinning. Adolf took the grouse and started pulling off feathers. Cokey handed Oskar a cup of coffee and then helped Sven cut up the deer. After finishing his cofee, Oskar started building the fire to cook their supper.

The next morning the four buddies sat in their saddles and watched the morning's parade of mustang herds. A large red dun stallion followed a nice group of over fifty mares, colts and yearlings towards the water. Adolf said, "This is the one. There is healthy stock in that herd and it is of a good size. That big paint out front is the lead mare. If we push her toward our pen and split others away from her, they will be confused. I reckon it should work."

When they saw the paint leading the herd back, they split the herd. Cokey and his cutting horse forced the big mare towards the gate of their pen, while Adolf and Oskar split part of the herd away. Sven kept the other group following Cokey and the lead mare. The red dun stallion came flying at them with teeth bared and neck stretched out. Adolf dodged him and Oskar rode in waving a rolled lariat in front of the stallion. The red dun took off after the group of mares and colts that were escaping. He stopped once as if he wanted to come back for the group Sven and Cokey were turning into the pen, but decided to keep the fleeing group in sight and rode after them.

Adolf and Oskar joined their other two friends to help keep the captured horses moving into the pen, but were not needed; the group was used to following the herd matriarch. They dismounted and pulled the gate rails into the opening. The big paint in the lead had slowed down at the other side and tried to push the rail down, but it held. The confused herd behind her was circling around the pen looking for an opening. The paint ran around the pen and tried to go back through the gate but stopped when Cokey and Sven placed their mounts in front of the gate. It was hard to see the other mustangs because of the cloud of dust they were kicking up, but the constant wind was blowing the cloud away fairly rapidly.

Gradually, the herd started settling down and only their leader was still looking for an opening. Finally, she gave in and settled down herself. She stood and glared at the four men to let them know she thought they were evil. She stood about thirty feet from them, standing sideways and whining to tell them she was damn not impressed.

Adolf spoke up, "I count twenty-nine, including nine colts and two older mares we won't keep. I think that will be a good start. Once these settle down, we'll do this again and should have enough to give us a start."

"I'll cut the older mares out in a while," Cokey said as he dismounted. He put a foot on the bottom rail and his chin on top of his arms on the top rail.

Adolf was watching the paint, "Do you think we should turn her loose? I'm not sure she can be settled down and may be too much trouble."

"I think you may have a point," Oskar said as he walked over to stand next to Adolf. "I sure don't want to have her chasing me around that darn pen. She scares me some."

"I reckon you scare mighty easy like," chuckled Cokey, "A damn sissy girl I do reckon." He trotted over behind Sven to ensure Oskar wasn't coming after him, and made faces at Sven.

Cokey mounted his mustang and separated the two older mares plus one mare's colt. Adolf rode his gelding to keep the three separated. Cokey then took on the dangerous job of separating the lead mare. She finally headed for the gate and Sven and Oskar slid it open. The paint flew through it like a jackrabbit being chased by a coyote. The two older mares and the colt were right on her tail as they ran for home.

They repeated their process the next day and added another twenty-three mustangs to the twenty-five from the first day. That evening they made a better gate using rawhide as hinges. They used a hemp rope to make a circle latch they could drop over a fence post. The gate overlapped the fence on the inside so it could only be opened inward; to ensure the mustangs couldn't push the gate open.

The familiarization process started the next morning. They took turns riding slowly amongst the wild horses, getting them to accept their presence. By the second day, the mustangs ignored them as they rode around, talking to the mustangs. The third day, Adolf dismounted and walked around the corral leading Buck. Then the other three men did the same with their mounts. By the fourth day the herd had accepted the men being in the pen with them and even let the men touch them without flinching. The colts became curious and would come to the men to accept grass and then wild carrots from their hands. This caused some of the mares to become brave enough to come get the carrots too.

Over the next few days, more and more of the mares became used to having their noses rubbed, even though the men had to be ready to avoid being nipped. Next they started getting the horses used to having a blanket laid across their back, and eventually a lariat around their necks.

By the time they were ready to trail the herd to their meadow, a few of the mares were trained to be led on a rope behind Sven and his stallion. They led the herd from the corral and headed for their valley. The herd fell in line behind Sven and the three mares he was leading, while the other three men kept any mustangs from trying to escape, although none did. They all had the herd mentality.

They spent the next month in their valley working with the mares that did not have any colts. At month's end had twenty mustangs ready to sell to Major Hitchcock. They had made geldings out of all the male colts and yearlings. These they were going to teach to be ridden and eventually sold.

They also started the process for building their ranch. They used the large two handled saws to cut ponderosa pine and the mules to drag the logs to the building site. They built the bunkhouse first, including a stone fireplace on the north wall. They notched each log eighteen inches from each end to interlock with the perpendicular walls. The logs were all alternated so the large ends were opposite of their neighbors. The second from the top logs were top-notched every three feet and beams notched and place on top for the roof. The top log was placed to hold the beams down and three foot planks were made with their broad ax to make the roof. They cutout spaces for two widows on the east side and made hand hewn two-inch thick shutters using rawhide for hinges.

Sven had Cokey mixing adobe to use to hold the stone together for the fireplace and chimney, "Get your skinny butt in gear. I'm wasting time for you to mix my mud. Will be nigh on winter if you don't scramble those bowed legs of yours."

When the bunkhouse was completed, they started moving from the tent. "Sure will be nice sleeping inside tonight," said Oskar as he placed his bedroll on the rough plank floor. He dropped his possibles on the floor and said, "Tomorrow I'll hammer together some beds so we can sleep off the floor." Then he headed to the tent to grab some more stuff to move over.

Chapter 31

"Sven, come take a looksee." Oskar was standing with one of the windows open, looking towards the east end of the meadow. "Indians are at the gate."

As Sven looked out the window, Oskar went to the door and hollered at Adolf, who was rubbing the nose of a very happy colt. He pointed with his chin to the east and Adolf saw the Indians. Adolf walked over to the spring to get Cokey's attention, "Hey, seems we got company. Walk slowly to the bunkhouse." Adolf walked back to the colt as Cokey meandered to the bunkhouse to join Oskar and Sven. The two already had their rifles in hand and Sven was standing by a window. When Cokey got inside he picked up his rifle and hurried to the other window. Oskar carried Adolf's big .54 out to Adolf and stood beside him in the yard. They faced the five Indians peering over their gate.

"Hold steady until they let us know what they are up to," Adolf ordered. He held his Hawkens across his arms and walked a couple of steps towards the Indians, then raised his right hand with the palm out. "Sven, place my shotgun just outside the door in case they rush us. The way they're dressed I think them to be the Utes Major Hitchcock told me about." He noticed the Indians weren't showing an open hand so he whispered to Oskar, "Lay your rifle by me and get Buck and Patches in case they try for the herd."

"Will do," Oskar whispered. He laid his Kentucky rifle by Adolf's left foot, turned and trotted west of the bunkhouse where the riding horses were grazing. He put the reins on his and Adolf's geldings and led them back to Adolf. "I got them," he told Adolf as he came up behind him.

One of the Indians kicked his pinto and let out a, *"Hi-eeee-aaa."* He rode toward the mustang herd with obvious intent, so Adolf brought his Hawkens to his shoulder and followed the Indian with the barrel until he was in range. The rifle sound echoed throughout the meadow as the wounded brave threw his arms up toward the blue sky and fell off the pinto pony. The sound of fleeing birds filled the air.

Adolf spun to grab the mane of Buck and pulled himself aboard. Grabbing the reins, he yelled, "Come on. We need to protect our herd from them thieves."

Oskar was already on Patches and following as he knew what his friend would do. "I'm here," the man of many words knew when to limit his output. His Colt Paterson appeared in his right hand as he gripped the reins in his left.

The four remaining Utes had applied their heels to their ponies' flanks and were heading toward their fallen comrade. All were yelling that same shrill, *"Hi-eeee-aaa."*

"Don't shoot unless I do," Adolf yelled to the bunkhouse. "You too," he told Oskar as they raced to keep the Indians from the mustang herd. Adolf was mistaken in thinking that, if they acted friendly toward the Indians, they could live peacefully.

The herd had reacted to the echoing gunshot and trotted away from the shrill yells of the charging Indians. They picked up speed as the Indians rode toward them, making it easier for Adolf and Oskar to get between the horses and the Indians. The Indians started sending arrows towards the young men.

"Damn it!" yelled Adolf as one of the arrows struck his left thigh. He raised Mr. Paterson and let fly a couple shots. Oskar fired three quick shots. They were close enough to the bunkhouse that two rifle shots joined the battle. Two of the braves were hit. One slumped over the arched neck of his black and white paint and fled for the gate. The second almost fell from his blue dun pony, but one of the other warriors pushed him back up. They followed the first rider. The last brave glared at Adolf and Oskar, but turned back toward the first wounded Indian and pulled him onto the back of his horse, the rider-less pinto followed them. Just like that it was over and the meadow was peaceful again.

Sven walked into the bunkhouse carrying the clippers he used on horseshoe nails. He walked over to Adolf, who was lying on his bed with his left leg propped up on his bedroll, an arrow pointing to the ceiling. "These pinchers should snip through the arrow easily. One of you holds that arrow still so I don't hurt him. Someone boil an old shirt or something for when we get that damn arrow out of him."

They let the hole bleed some, after removing the arrow, to get the impurities out. They placed the boiled shirt on it for a while and then packed a thick bunch of moss on both holes and tightly wrapped the leg.

"I thought if we only wounded them and let them pick up their wounded they would realize we don't want to harm them," Adolf was explaining to the others why he had let the buckskin clad warriors go.

Cokey was shaking his head. He rubbed the stubble on his chin as he argued with himself whether he should speak up or hold his peace. After all he was the new comer, but he decided truth was the best route. "Don't rightly agree with you. I reckon they be similar to the Comanche in Texas. They see it as a weakness, not a kindness, if you don't kill them." He figured he was not near as smart as Adolf so he kept his head down with his hands tucked in his belt, "Sure don't want to upset you, but we should of kilt them dead and hid the carcasses."

Adolf gave Cokey a long look, and then he looked off to the ceiling like he wanted to have a life do-over, "Figure you're right. Dang it all! I hate killing, even if it be an Indian. Why can't we all let each other alone?"

Oskar patted his long time friend's shoulder, "Always admired your gentle side, Adolf. I am figuring Cokey is right and we have to change for this new, wild country. All of us need to be harder out here if we want to survive. What do you think Sven?"

"I don't like killing, but I sure don't want you alls to be killed. I had to force myself to kill for food and have a notion this is another way to grow up. I fear those wild Injuns are going to collect friends and come back for our mustangs and our scalps. You betcha. That's what I think."

"You guys are damn right. I sure do hate it but I got to pull up my big boy britches and become a man." With that Adolf laid his head down and covered his eyes with his arms. "Leave me alone for a while. I need to think on this."

All three of the men stopped at the door to look back at their leader, lying wounded on his lonely bed with his arms over his eyes. They all knew that their friend was extremely sensitive and needed to wrap his mind around their discussion. Then each quietly trooped out to commence with their never-ending chores.

Chapter 32

A couple of coyotes were arguing in the night about who was better looking and had bragging rights to impress the uninterested bitch coyotes. The dummies were ignorant, like most males. The females were just looking for food to take home to their puppies. A very beautiful night at the edge of the Rocky Mountains had settled over the budding ranch. Millions of stars fought for space in the heavens above. The makeshift door of the bunkhouse was hanging open to allow the young pioneers to appreciate the cooling night breeze. Of course, the continuous Kansas Territory winds were coming from the west in undulating waves, undecided as to the volume that it should blow. Also open were the shutters on the windows, as evidenced by their constant banging.

The four men were stripped down to only their underwear bottoms as a means to combat the warm night. A gentle fire was burning in the fireplace, not for additional heat, but only to boil another pot of black coffee. Adolf was sitting up in bed and Oskar was sitting cross-legged on the next bed. Sven and Cokey were lounging on the floor. Tanned faces were a severe contrast to the paleness of their bodies, except for Oskar. In his case his face was red, since it never tanned, but both his face and his fish white body were covered with thousands of freckles.

The friends were engrossed in a thoughtful discussion of tasks still needed to construct their ranch – a continuation of several days' exchange of thoughts and ideas. Adolf's leg was healing nicely and he had been limping around without a crutch for the past few days. No

Indians had appeared in the three weeks since that first attempt to steal horses.

The ranch owners had built a three rail fence parallel to the river. The gate was moved to the west end, just north of the bunkhouse. They hoped this would make it harder for hooligans trying to invade their meadow. It was also used to ensure the mustangs didn't wander over to the Cache la Poudre and fall in, especially the curious colts. It had taken a lot of hard work sweating under the blistering sun, but they were pleased with the result. They had traveled several more times to the location of the wild mustangs, where they now referred to as Mustang Valley. They now had an estimated one hundred to sell, in addition to the sizable number of brood mares and colts they had selected for their own starter herd. All the male colts had been castrated and seemed to be healthy and unaware their future had forever been altered. The yearling males had won the lottery and remained with their nuts intact, since they were to be sold.

Their next projects were to dig a root cellar to store their winter supplies and to build a strong shed to cut and hang meat. They were also going to build a small, temporary pole barn to protect their riding horses from the elements. Sven's knowledge of cold snowy Minnesota winters was a caution that they did not know what to expect for weather in this Kansas Territory. Just to be safe, he had suggested they travel out to the prairie to gather grass to store as a backup. They all thought this to be a good idea and were planning to sharpen their new sickles and harvest some of the tall prairie grass on the eastern range.

Sven and Cokey had made a trip the previous week to Fort John with a couple of mules for supplies and discovered that a man named Harley

(Perk) Perkins had opened a sawmill by Fort John. Adolf suggested taking the mustangs to the fort to sell and make arrangements to order sawed wood to use for building their barn. Since Sven was familiar with building barns, he had been nominated to design theirs, which was to include a loft for storing hay.

Talking about the future, Adolf said, "I think we can hold off on building the house and barn until next summer, but we should gather lumber all winter."

"Ya betcha," said Sven. "We need to let the cut trees cure. Green wood will shrink and cause us all kinds of headaches." They had already accepted his idea to square the logs for a large, multi-room house. Sven had shown how he used a broad head ax to slice the sides off. They were already aware that in the seventeen hundreds the Swedish settlers along the Delaware River had introduced to the new country how to build both log cabins and the larger log houses. Sven's family had brought their simple building tools, consisting of ax, adz, and auger, across the ocean. Sven had helped build several structures in Minnesota.

"Old Charlie Clemens did build with green lumber in Ohio," stated Oskar. "Adolf, remember how his crooked house shifted and sprung gaps? Every rainfall pranced right on in." Then he aimed a finger at Sven, "I sure am pleased you plan to avoid a leaky house."

Adolf added, "I do remember and also remember all the logs that cracked wide open when they dried." He smiled at the memory and said, "Now that was a real disaster."

Cokey had a strange look on his face and had been unusually quiet for the discussion. "Partners, I being from Texas have never experienced this snow you is talking about. Why is ya'all so damn feared of it?"

Oskar reached down for his boot and threw it at Cokey, "Buddy you sure are going to experience something new and your skinny little butt is going to have icicles hanging downwards."

"Ufta," bellowed Sven as he wrapped his massive arms around Cokey. "Old man, you are going to get woken up to a happening." He pushed Cokey away and said, "Golly gee, you are going to be crying like a baby for old man winter to get out of here. Don't come bawling to me when your teeny pecker freezes solid."

Rolling around his bed laughing, Oskar takes another turn, "Let's all bet on when this old man starts bellyaching about the cold or gets stuck in the outhouse, afraid of putting his little feets in the cold snow."

Reliably, Adolf was more serious, "We'll have to make sure he knows how to dress for the cold. I would not have thought of that." But, then, he also was grinning ear to ear.

Adolf spoke up again, "I been thinking."

Oskar said, "No kidding. How unusual, huh guys?" He grinned at his good friend to ensure he knew he was joking.

Adolf pretended to swing a fist at his friend and continued, "We were lucky we saw those Indians." He looked at each one in turn and said, "We need a warning system of some kind."

Oskar knew his best friend was right, "Got any ideas, Adolf?"

Adolf scratched his elbow where a mosquito had just bit him, "I think we should get some dogs. What do you all think?"

Sven was nodding his head as he answered, "You damn betcha. We need some barking friends that will get our attention."

"How are we going to come onto dogs?" asked Cokey, as he stood up and refilled his tin cup with warm java. He stopped and picked a splinter from his left foot before carrying the steaming coffee pot to refill Oskar's cup.

"Now that's real easy-like," spoke Oskar, "Those Injuns at the fort had lots of barkers." He smiled real big, "Some of those trapper fellas had big mutts trailing behind them."

Sven was being quiet and thoughtful. "I got a second idea. We should hook up some metal triangles to bang on. If ones of us spies Injuns we can warn all of the others."

"I think that is one splendid idea," Adolf said. "Remember how we had to try to get each other's attention when those feathered riders first arrived?" He clapped his hands, "Thanks big buddy. Think you can hammer together some for us?"

"Ya betcha I can," Sven looked proud his idea had gained acceptance.

As Adolf drifted to sleep, he told himself, "These are damn good partners. They work well together - a team to ride the river with. They all contribute without any infighting." He sent a silent prayer to God and switched his mind to thoughts of his lovely Caroline.

Chapter 33

The first natural change to the valley occurred in late summer – the grass succumbed to the constant dry heat winds and abandoned the color green in favor of a duller gold. No other changes developed until early October, when the deciduous trees had the notion to start changing out of their green summer clothes. The aspens' leaves turned a brilliant yellow and the willows and elms copied with their own shades of yellow. To the surprise of the four partners, brilliant reds sprouted throughout the hills, denoting various types of maple trees.

"We need to remember where the maples are hanging out. We can tap them for syrup next fall," Sven told them. "Probably too late for the sap to be running, but next year we will have tasty syrup for pancakes."

A few weeks later the majestic granddaddy oaks joined the fashion parade by slipping into their fall coats of purple. Of course, the stubborn evergreens stayed green, providing a contrast for nature's colorful collage.

On an early November night, an evil elf carrying a magic icicle wand of cold snuck into the meadow and the next morning the trees were naked and shivering in the frigid wind. It was almost Thanksgiving before the men got their first taste of snow, but it was only enough to provide a white layer on top of the grass and clinging to the evergreens. The two days before the snow fell, the constant wind had turned cold as a prelude to the brief storm. The morning following the storm, the good fairy sprinkled her enchanted dust over the land and the temperature became so warm they didn't need jackets and the snow was just a memory.

The loud banging of metal on metal startled Adolf, but he reacted by looking to the east where a large group of mounted Indians wearing war paint were grouped. He dashed into the bunk house and grabbed all the rifles and his long shotgun. Running for the door, he almost collided with Oskar. With a determined look, Oskar said, "Sven and Cokey are with some colts by the spring. I clanged the warning and saw they are riding towards us. Take a window and I will meet the boys with their rifles. Throw me their ammunition pouches. 'Kay?" He grabbed the three Kentucky Long Rifles and the pouches Adolf threw at him.

Adolf opened the shutter on one of the east windows and arranged himself for battle. A couple of the braves were using tomahawks to chop at a couple of the rails, but it was taking them some time to drop the top two rails. He heard horses slide to a stop and Oskar yelling instructions to the new arrivals.

By then the war party was galloping towards them, but the distance was still close to a mile, way too far for Adolf to fire his Hawkens. The new ranch mustangs had raised their heads and started drifting to the west to get away from the movement of the Indians. But the Indians were ignoring the herd and heading straight for the bunkhouse. The shrill war cries were coming into range as the war party tried to put fear into the heads of the white men.

Cokey ran through the door and opened the shutters for the second window, "Them warning triangles sure got our attention. I am plumb happy that Sven hung 'em for us." As he laid out powder and ball, he added, "You yell to me what to do and I gets her done."

Adolf had the big Hawkens aimed to the Indians, "We'll take turns firing. That way we won't get caught both unloaded. I'll fire first when they are still out too far for you. I'll reload and fire again, then you can shoot when they are in your range."

"Good enough for me. Hope we save the horses and our scalps."

"Where are the others setting up?" Adolf glanced over to Cokey. He felt protective of everyone and wasn't comfortable with them out of sight. "There are so many we need to stick together."

"They rolled the wagon over by the door to use." Cokey let out a giggle, "I am downright scared enough to piss my pants, but somewhat excited to fight alongside you all."

Adolf remembered the conversation after the last attack so he spoke up, "Remember we decided to kill them, so aim at their chests." He asked forgiveness from the Lord for what they were going to do. He noticed the Utes were wearing animal skin shirts and pants and their ponies were painted and decorated with feathers. He took aim at the lead rider, held his breath, and slowly squeezed the trigger. The big .54 responded and sent the large ball across the meadow to slam into its target. The brave tossed his hands to the sky and dropped off his pony as it veered away. Adolf quickly reloaded and sent another brave to chase the first to the happy hunting ground.

As he reloaded again, he heard two shots cut loose outside and looked up in time to watch two more Indians bite the dust. Cokey's Kentucky musket discharged, filling the air with black smoke and hot lead to knock another brave from his horse. By then Adolf heard a hailstorm of thunks as arrows hit the thick logs of the bunkhouse. Within a beat of his heart, the world turned to chaos as the battle erupted. Adolf's focus shrunk to his immediate targets. The pellets shot from the ten gauge hammered into a group of braves, shredding men and horses into pieces of white bone, red blood, and copper flesh. His second shot devastated anyone within its spread pattern. By then the popping of pistols were dropping braves left and right, his pistol included. Out of his right eye he saw a brave fall with an ax stuck in his chest. Preparing for hand to hand confrontation, he pulled out his tomahawk and belt knife, but the Indians were in full retreat.

Adolf yelled, "Reload everyone." He got off a final shot with the Hawkens before they were out of range but missed. He watched the war party ride back through the new gap in the fence followed by several riders-less ponies, disappearing through the valley entrance. He took the time to pull the barrel of his Colt open, remove the cylinder, and reload. He thought to himself, "It takes too damn long to reload these pistols".

Adolf ran to the door to check on Oskar and Sven and found them in the wagon prepared for another charge. "Any one hurt?"

"Just some scratches. Nothing serious. How about you guys?"

"We're fine," Adolf answered as he looked at all the arrows sticking into the ground and wagon. He walked around the corner and saw the same multitude of arrows sticking into the bunkhouse wall. Off to the east the meadow was spotted with Indian bodies and some ponies. A few of the ponies were screaming in pain and thrusting hooves in the air. Hanging above the wagon and drifting from the windows of the bunkhouse were black clouds and the smell of burnt gunpowder irritated his nose.

Oskar jumped out of the wagon and said, "We need to check to see if any of the Injuns are breathing."

Adolf nodded his head and went inside for his shotgun and a handful of shells. He walked to the bodies with the hammers of his shotgun pulled back, Oskar beside him with his pistol cocked. They stopped for Oskar to fire a shot into the three damaged horses, but found no Indian alive. The battleground was sickening to Adolf, all those lost lives. As he got to the last body, he relaxed a little but then gagged, dropped to his knees, and heaved breakfast onto the ground. In the background he heard Oskar throwing up also. "I hate this," thought Adolf. He turned his head to the rumbling of Sven and Cokey bringing the wagon out to them.

Without a word, they started heaping the Indian carcasses into the wagon. Adolf refused to count them, he did not want to know how many they were responsible for killing. They also gathered up the weapons and colorfully painted shields to put into the wagon.

The bunkhouse was quiet that night as each man relived the battle. Adolf finally spoke up, "It takes too damn long to reload these Paterson's. They give us five rapid shots then we don't have time to go through the process of pulling the barrel forward, taking out the cylinder, loading powder and ball, replacing caps and then putting the gun together again." He shook his head and got up to walk the floor. "They give us lots of firepower, but then we are left with hand to hand fighting, without guns." He looked at his nodding friends, "We got to find a fix or get more guns."

Oskar spoke up, "Sure can't afford buying more. Too damn spendy, Adolf my man."

Adolf said, "Not as spendy as dying."

Cokey looked around, then spoke out, "We done did kilt a lot of them just now."

"Yes we did, but that's mostly because of our defensive location. They had to travel a mile across the open, so we shot several before they were close enough to use their bows. Then they shot their arrows damn fast but our pistols were fast too. But when our guns were empty, they were still shooting arrows. Heaven forbid they ever start the battle closer." Adolf was downright serious about his concern.

Chapter 34

A few days later Adolf was working with a striped-back dun palomino colt, getting it used to a saddle. He was gently putting the saddle on then taking it off, and repeating the process over and over. Oskar was a few feet away going through the same process with a spunky red dun; the dun kept reaching back to pull the saddle blanket off as if this was a game, like some school boy acting up in the classroom. Adolf was trying hard to keep a snicker hidden as his boyhood friend became more and more frustrated. Served him right for all the teachers Oskar had irritated with his daily pranks.

The day was starting out very pleasant. The fluffy white clouds were acting chameleon-like by changing shapes to items limited only by one's imagination. The constant wind was softer today and carried a slight coolness that required light jackets in spite of the sweaty work. Adolf was watching a cloud shaped like a deer transform into a happy faced puppy as it bounded eastward. He caught movement at the entrance to their meadow. His first reaction was to panic and run to clang the closest triangle, but the color blue triggered a soothing response. His closer inspection provided comfort as he watched a troop of soldiers riding two abreast. "Oskar, looks like the army is coming to visit."

Oskar was in the midst of picking up the blanket from the ground and didn't catch what Adolf had said. "What was that you said?" He turned to face Adolf as he continued, "I was just a might busy with this ornery beast. I am thinking seriously about grilling horse steaks tonight."

"I said we got visitors." Adolf quickly said more when he saw Oskar start to become alarmed, "It's some army folks." He pointed towards the riders as they approached the gate.

Oskar looked where Adolf was indicating and asked, "Wonder what brings them here." He removed his rumpled hat and ran his hand through his sweat-soaked red hair.

"Bet we're about to find out," answered Adolf. The soldiers had opened the gate and were coming toward them. Adolf smiled when he recognized Major Hitchcock up front. "Let's go gab." He led the palomino toward the new arrivals.

"Do you reckon they are upset 'bout us squatting in Injun territory?" Oskar put his hand on Adolf's arm to slow him up.

"Nah. The major and I talked about that and he was in agreement." Adolf started walking again with Oskar right beside him.

The troop of about thirty galloped forward and stopped by Adolf and Oskar. "Welcome Major. Sure surprised seeing you here." Adolf pointed behind him and added, "There's a cold spring over there. Have your men quench their thirst and that of their mounts."

"I thank you. We sure could use that. The ride got us parched." Hitchcock turned his head to the sergeant behind him and said, "Sergeant Hennessy, dismount the men and fall out for a drink of water."

"Troop dismount!" the bearded soldier with three yellow stripes on both arms of his blue wool jacket bellowed. When they were dismounted he ordered, "Fall out for a water break."

"We do have a couple pitchers of cold tea sitting in the spring, if you care to join me," Adolf said. He took his hat off, removed the halter from the skittish colt, and patted it on its rump to send it toward its mom. He then reached his hand out to shake with the army officer, "What brings you to our meadow?"

The major was wiping the sweat from the back of his neck with a yellow bandana as he said, "A couple of scouts rode into the fort and said they saw a large war party of Utes down this way. I figured you were the only ones they would be after. Don't know of any Cheyenne or Arapaho villages this close so I thought we better check it out." He led his horse over to the spring surrounded with his men.

"We sure appreciate your concern. We were attack by a large band, whooping and hollering." He looked down to his feet as he added, "We did kill a bunch of them. Hated doing that, but I hope they got the message and stay away."

"This area is not that important to the Utes but they just don't like intruders." The commander looked Adolf in the eyes, "You must have been ready for them. Huh?"

Adolf pointed at the iron triangle hanging from the bunkhouse. "We came up with the idea to set those up as a warning to each other. If anyone spots Indians, we beat the hell out of one of those noise makers." He nodded his head as he remembered the attack, "It sure did work and we had a good amount of time to watch them charge over that open ground."

"Pretty damn smart if you ask me." Major Hitchcock stopped to stare at the huge herd of mustangs, "My God! Look at all those steeds." He looked shocked, "You guys sure didn't let the grass grow under your feet. Have you got any horses to sell yet?"

Adolf followed the major's gaze, "Reckon we got over a hundred, green broke and ready for you." He stuck his hands inside the top of his pants, "We were leery about trailing them to the fort. Afraid the Indians would come back while we were gone."

Major Hitchcock said, "We can help you there. We can herd them back for you and pay you when you next come to the fort."

Just then Sven and Cokey rode in. The major said, "Is this the rest of your group?"

"Sure is. Come meet them."

"Good gracious! That's the biggest man I have ever seen," Hitchcock exclaimed at the sight of Sven.

Adolf introduced his two partners. Hitchcock looked at the two new comers and started laughing, "Does anyone get you two mixed up?"

This brought a smile to the ranchers. With a straight face, Cokey spoke up, "Nah. Any fool can see I'm the good looking fellow and he's the ugly brute." Then he bent over and slapped his knee, erupting in laughter at his own joke. Sven just grinned good naturedly.

Oskar joined them and met the officer also. "I was just calculating that you all might be hungry. Want me to burn some venison for you all? We got enough to feed your whole troop."

"Now that is right friendly, but we don't want to eat up all your food."

Sven giggled like a ten year old, "We loves to hunt and this ole valley is heaped full of animals."

"Well that is polite. We got the fixings for throwing together lots of biscuits, if you will let us."

The soldiers had removed the bits from their horses' mouths so they could enjoy the grass wearing its golden fall color, and were lounging around in conversation groups.

Adolf was filling in Major Hitchcock on how the mustangs had been trained. "I would consider them to be green broken. They may be a little skittish, but they have all been ridden."

"Very interesting. I am used to seeing them broken by bucking them into the ground." He was looking over at the large mustang herd. "Would like to go look them over and start rounding them up."

Chapter 35

Two days later an enormous cloud of blowing dust announced the arrival of the herd to Fort John. Gawking hoards of Indians collected to watch the herd of mustangs being driven by the soldiers – all covered by so much trail powder that it was impossible to see their blue uniforms, especially those riding drag. The wild horses seemed aware they were causing a spectacle and galloped with their heads held high - as if they too were soldiers on parade. Even the other soldiers and buckskin clad trappers rushed over to watch this novelty, creating an atmosphere of a special holiday.

Bouncing along in front were Oskar and Adolf, driving their wagon as if they represented a marching band. They parked the wagon by the trading post as the drivers directed the mustangs into the post's corrals. The rail fence quickly sprouted excited spectators marveling at the multitude of different colored mustangs waltzing around the pen. The horses seemed to be enjoying the fuss they were creating. The troop of men that had brought them to the fort quickly dismounted and took care of their own mounts while arguing about which of the B words was to come first, a bath or a beer? All settled on the beer.

Oskar and Adolf joined the soldiers for a beer. They stood beside the major while Adolf loudly thanked the dust covered soldiers for bringing the horses in.

Everyone raised their beers and shouted, "Cheers."

"I counted 110. Is that your count?" The officer directed his question to Adolf.

"Yes. That is the same count I got."

Major Hitchcock pulled a stub of a pencil from his pocket and used a thumbnail to trim wood from around the lead. He licked the lead and scribbled on the back of an envelope from a pocket on his blouse. Oskar grinned at Adolf because he knew Adolf had already calculated the sum in his head. Adolf kept his face passive so as not to embarrass their military tablemate.

"I figure one thousand six hundred and fifty dollars." The major said as he looked up from his math work.

Adolf simply nodded.

The officer smiled, pleased he had not made a mistake. "Let's go to my office and get you fine gents the money you got coming, along with a shot of aged bourbon to seal our deal."

Adolf and Oskar followed the officer to his office and sat in a couple of rickety camp chairs. He pulled money from a locked desk drawer and counted out their payment. In the pile were a few twenty dollar bills, the rest of it consisted of tens and fives, making it an impressive pile of money. Adolf asked, "Have you a sack or something to put this in?"

"Sure do," the major answered. He picked up a couple of grain sacks that he was using for laundry and handed them to Adolf. Adolf tried to ignore the horrible stink of dirty socks drifting from the sacks as he split the pile of bills, putting some in each bag. Then he handed one to Oskar.

The major grabbed a bottle of amber liquid and three tumblers from his desk. He filled each glass with three fingers of bourbon and pushed a drink towards each of the others. He smiled like a Cheshire cat and held his glass up, "Here is to a long and successful relationship."

As they sat sipping on the smooth aged alcohol, Adolf said, "I got another subject that you may be able to help us resolve." He looked at Oskar and then leaned forward in his chair. "We have determined we need some dogs to warn us if someone sneaks into our ranch. Do you know of any we might obtain?"

The major rubbed his chin and then perked up, "I think I can help you. There are plenty of yappers with the Indians, but maybe the sergeant major knows of others. He knows everything going on about this post." He stepped to the office door and said, "Sergeant O'Malley would you step in here for a moment?"

After explaining the situation to the spick and span sergeant, he sat back and gazed at the tall noncom.

Sergeant O'Malley twisted one tip of his mustache in thought, before bursting out broad grin, "You younguns are in luck. A trapper found some unusual dog-like animal pups and brought them to the post yesterday. If you would follow me I can show them to you."

Adolf and Oskar exchanged looks wondering what 'dog-like' meant.

Oskar and Adolf shook hands with Major Hitchcock and let him go to his awaiting bath. They followed the big noncom to an area behind the trading post. Approaching a group of grimy buckskinned unkempt trappers, they were startled by a gunshot followed by a yelp of an animal in pain. Adolf burst forward in long strides followed by his redhead friend. The sergeant major hesitated before chasing after them.

Adolf plowed through the crowd and slid to a stop in front of a large cage. The cage contained five very large puppies – one dead, one wounded, and three cowing in one corner. A second shot ended the life of the wounded puppy to the sound of excited laughing.

"What the hell are you doing?" Adolf shouted as he yanked the smoking pistol from the filthy hand of a large, smelly mountain man. He obviously had neither shaved nor bathed in at least the last two centuries. The trapper tried to retrieve his gun, but stopped when he looked into the piercing gray eyes of a very angry Adolf.

"These are mine animals." He pointed to a scrawny gray haired man of less than five feet who was standing at the back of the crowd with a disgusted look. "Crazy Jake sold alls them to me for twenty five cents, a nickel each. Must be some wild animal related to a wolf from their size."

"You ignorant asshole. Those are puppies, just babies," growled Adolf.

Some of the crowd started to slink off, but the others started to crowd closer and pull out large knives. They stopped with the hammer click of a pistol. Oskar had placed his Colt Paterson at the back of the head of the trapper standing behind Adolf. Adolf was confident Oskar had his back and didn't look around.

During that hesitation from the crowd, a loud commanding voice boomed, "You all better step your damn hides away from them boys or I will have all of you hanged after I cuts your dicks off." Sergeant Major O'Malley strode forward with his gloved hands behind his back and his commanding eyes challenging every man there to disobey him. Some privates had heard the commotion and at the sound of their sergeant's loud voice they triple-stepped over to surround the group, with rifles cocked. The mountain men disappeared like a magician's vanishing act.

"Thank you sergeant O'Malley." Adolf grabbed the shooter by his buckskins before he could step away. He threw three nickels on the ground, "I just bought those puppies. Any argument?"

"They're yours," the trapper picked up the coins without looking away from Adolf. He flinched so violently when Adolf stepped forward that he fell on his butt and slid away without rising.

O'Malley scratched his head, "I do not know what breed them dogs are. Are they a wild dog cousin or part wolf?"

Oskar had opened the cage and spoke up, "Damn, look at this Adolf. These am some of those big Irish Wolfhounds like old man Reilly brought over from Europe. Look at their paws. They are going to be really big hounds." The puppies had square heads, wire-like gray and brindle hair, and long tails that were pounding the ground like housewives beating the dust from rugs. Oskar was holding up one's paw, which was already bigger than that of most full grown dogs. "They done have to grow to fit these oversized paws." He giggled like a kid when all three puppies proceeded to lick his face, "These guys are trying to slurp off mine freckles, yes they are. Heh, heh."

The friends thanked Sergeant Major O'Malley. The little trapper referred to as Crazy Jack had stayed around and approached the two friends. "Thankee, sure didn't think Gumbo Pete was planning to kill them dogs. I am downright disgusted with him and won't allow him to my campfire ever again." He took a long look at the dogs, shook his head, and walked sadly away.

Adolf and Oskar removed the oversized puppies from the cage, watered them, and placed them in their wagon. They fed the puppies several pieces of beef jerky, which were devoured instantly.

They drove the wagon over to the sawmill and picked up some of the planks they had ordered for their barn. After paying the Mr. Perkins and arranging to pick up the rest of their lumber in the spring, they started south. Oskar was playing with two of the puppies while the male kept trying to crawl onto Adolf's lap. Although Adolf pretended to be stern, he had a grin ear to ear and sneaked a hand to pet the puppy when he thought Oskar wasn't looking.

"When these grow full size they going to fit Sven, I do think," Oskar said again as they entered the trail alongside of the river. By this time the male was lying with his head in Adolf's lap and the other two were arguing over who had the right to sit on Oskar's lap. It was hard to tell which were the happiest, the men or the puppies.

Chapter 36

By the end of the week, a routine had settled in. The two bitch dogs, Ginger and Rascal, got in everyone's way, and their significant tails had left bruises all over Sven and Oskar. They seemed to detect that Cokey was somewhat leery of them and were less rambunctious with him. On the other hand, the male named Quinn was totally devoted to Adolf. He had given up trying to crawl into Adolf's bed at night, but slept right beside it on a blanket. He had stolen Adolf's pillow and the boys were surprised when Adolf let him keep it. It had become common to see Quinn within a couple of feet of his new master.

At first, all of the horses were skittish of the playful puppies. After a few days the puppies seemed to grasp the situation and settled down. The horses adapted to these new animals roaming amongst them. The men were very pleased with the deep-throated bark the puppies demonstrated. Cokey said, "Well now, we damn will hear those hollers. They are loud enough to wake my dead grandma all the way down in Texas."

It was obvious that the growing dogs seemed to understand their purpose. Early one morning the men were harshly brought out of their sleep by loud barking. All three dogs were scratching at the door. When Sven opened the door, they flew out; Quinn was in the lead with his littermates on his tail. It was light enough for the men to see a big cougar running to get out of this unfriendly neighborhood.

The half-grown dogs returned immediately at Oskar's command and smiled big, like expecting to be praised for their efforts – and they were.

Half-grown was somewhat of an understatement for these three pups. Quinn was upwards of a good hundred pounds and the girls were not much lighter. Quinn could almost place his paws on Adolf's shoulders and all three made Cokey look like a teeny-weeny boy.

Later in the year, the weather changed. Something in the air was disturbing the herd. They held their heads up high and trotted back and forth throughout the meadow, but the dogs weren't barking. The day had started with a chill and gotten colder through the day. All of the men had taken a turn to retrieve warmer jackets from the bunkhouse, but were still shivering. Adolf was taking furtive glances to the west, where the white clouds were being pushed aside by their angry, gray big brothers. There was no sign of thunder or lightning, but the clouds were tumbling over each other in an effort to charge full scale into the valley.

Sven had been busy using his broad ax to chop off bark, leaving forty foot long logs of roughly a foot and a half square. Adolf and Oskar were each using a long-handled claw peavey to rotate the logs for Sven. Cokey kept dashing in to remove the scrap wood and toss it to the pile for firewood. This process had gone smoothly for days and they had a couple of large stacks of square logs for their house's construction. Quinn was lying by the bunkhouse, keeping a watchful eye on Adolf, while Ginger was chasing Rascal. There was a bucket hanging from her mouth, like some kind of game of doggy tag of which only they knew the rules.

The tops of the trees were swaying as if trying to jerk themselves from their roots and join all the leaves taking a hike eastward. The wind had not only picked up, but was gusting so hard that the men had to lean to the west to keep from taking flight. Then, like a snap of a finger, the temperature plummeted, announcing that old man frost had come to visit. The two playing bitches took off to join Quinn at the bunkhouse door, using more intelligence than the four men were displaying.

Adolf glanced to make sure their mounts were in the corral and started to yell something, but instead got a mouthful of snow that had appeared from the mountains. Without a word, the young friends started a serious race to the bunkhouse, with bowlegged Cokey arriving last.

"Was it your bowed legs or your old age that slowed you down?" Oskar asked Cokey as he finally made it to the door and slammed it shut. "I was thinking you were going to be blown away with the leaves." He pushed Cokey towards his bed and burst out with a belly-rolling laugh.

Sven took on a serious look and said, "I do apologize to you old man. Just wasn't thinking fast enough, I wasn't. Hee, hee, I should have tucked you under my arm and carried you home." He exploded with laughter at his own joke as Cokey gave him a mighty scornful look.

"Ya all ain't funny at all. Just plain ole stupid." He turned his face quickly to keep them from seeing the grin on his own face.

"Now ufta. That sure all came along sudden like," Sven said. "Sure enough resembles one of those Minnesota blizzards which I thought I had left. Yah, Yah." He gave the biggest shiver any of them had ever seen and hurried to the fireplace to jam in several logs.

The blizzard lasted three days and dumped two feet of snow in the valley, but it wasn't evenly spread. The wind had played havoc with the placement of the white covering. Some places barely had three inches and others drifted eight feet high. One drift started at the northwest corner of the bunkhouse and walked right on over the top and slid down on the east side. The blowing wind had crusted the snow with a layer so solid that the three dogs walked up and over the building, leaving hardly a foot print.

All of the livestock had survived and the ice on the ponds was thin enough that the animals broke through very easily. Adam thought they might have to take hay out to feed them, but realized the mustangs were used to these conditions. The horses pawed through the shallow areas to uncover grass. Upon seeing this Sven said, "It sure isn't Minnesota. I've never seen snow flung about so much. But it is fun to look at, ya betcha."

Even the trees had got into dressing up for the winter scene. The pines were all wearing thick white winter coats and the leafless trees had a two-inch strip on their bare branches - like frosting on a cake. Although it was cold, it was nothing like the temperature during the blizzard. The sky looked no different than it did in summer – a brilliant azure without clouds to stop the sun from appearing happy.

The friends took turn shoveling paths to the privy, the spring, and the shed, as well as removing the snow from the corral and making sure the stream from the spring was flowing. They had to repeat everything when it snowed twice more.

Two weeks later the weather soared into the fifties and everything melted, which was great out in the pasture. But up in the yard, where the grass had been worn down, it became a quagmire. Mud several inches deep clung to their boots and made walking impossible. They tied forty-foot ropes to their five riding horses and staked them on the untouched grass north of the bunkhouse. They let the mules out to roam with the herd. A bench was built by the door to the bunkhouse, along with slats to scrape mud from their boots. They even left their boots at the door, but, still, spiteful gremlins tracked mud throughout their dwelling, some mud in the shape of dog paws.

Chapter 37

According to Adolf, January had slipped away and the month of
February had started its day by day march. Sven was obviously missing
Neale; several times a day he could be found looking to the east with a
face as long as an ax handle. "What if she forgets me?" he asked Adolf
one night.

"She won't," Adolf responded, but it caused him to wonder about his
own betrothed. It had been a year and a half since he had ridden away
from her crying in her mother's arms. He knew he still loved her, but
time has a way of mixing the mind up. Did he love her or just the
thought of loving her? What was love anyway? It was getting harder
and harder to remember her face or what it felt like to hold her in his
arms. If it was this troublesome for him, what was it like for her? She
had no control of when he would come for her. She was a very lovely
woman, but still so young. Would she succumb to the attention of some
other man? What if something had happened to her and he was not there
to protect her?

His thoughts were interrupted by the extremely loud barking of Quinn,
Ginger, and Rascal. They were putting up an awesome fuss. Adolf
quickly ran for a chime as he looked to the east. A dozen Indians in
buckskins were coming through the gap. As he grabbed the clangor rope
to strike the hanging triangle, something registered that caused him to
pause. Their hairstyle was not like the Utes. It was two braids with
eagle feathers hanging down, like that of the Cheyenne, and the warrior
in front was wearing a war bonnet in a similar fashion to their friend

Spirit Walking. Adolf clanged the bell to get his friends' attention, but was confident they were not being attacked.

The other three gathered around him with guns ready, but the Indian leader was holding his hand palm out as he rode along the fence. Adolf held his palm out also. All four relaxed when the Indians got to the gate; it was Spirit Walking.

The Indians slid off their pintos when they got to the men. Spirit Walking was smiling and jabbering a mile a minute. He motioned to one of the braves to join him and, when he did, the men saw that he was not an Indian. He was dressed like the rest, but his hair was light brown and his tanned face had a red tone rather than the copper of the others.

"I am Talking Owl. Spirit Walking has asked for me to repeat his words so you can understand." He was speaking in English! Spirit Walking started jabbering again and Talking Owl listened before speaking. Adolf did recognize Spirit Walking say 'Na-Gal'.

"Spirit Walking says he is happy to see you have your scalp," translated Talking Owl. Spirit Walking grinned at Adolf. "It is good that the spirits have looked over you and your braves."

Adolf said, "Tell him it pleases my heart to see Spirit Walking." Adolf motioned to the ground, "Will Spirit Walking smoke the pipe with us?"

It did not need a translation to understand Spirit Walking's response. He nodded his head and sat on a blanket one of the braves put on the ground.

"Tell him I will go get a pipe," Adolf told Talking Owl.

Spirit Walking shook his head and brought out the pipe Adolf had carved. He held it up and then pointed at Adolf's shirt pocket. Adolf grinned, pulled out his cherry-blend tobacco, and handed it to Spirit Walking.

Other blankets were laid down and everyone sat cross-legged in a large circle. The pipe was passed around. Many of the Indians raised their eyes in response to the taste, but Spirit Walking acted like it was old hat.

The Cheyenne had heard about the fight with their enemy, the Utes. Spirit Walking had decided to come tell Na-Gal that he was pleased. He also had heard that the Delaware were referring to Adolf as Kill-From-Afar. The Utes were repeating it as well, and referring to the four white men as Spirit Warriors. The Utes were advising their people to stay out of the valley, which was good news to the white men.

It appears that Spirit Walking had gained face amongst his tribe by being an ally to these white men. Other chiefs were treating him with much respect.

Talking Owl told them he had been twelve when he went with his pa, trapping in the mountains. A grizzly had killed his pa and the Cheyenne had found him and adopted him. Quinn walked over to sit by Adolf, and Ginger and Rascal sat by Oskar. Several of the Indians lunged to their feet and some even put their hands on the knives, but Spirit Walking pretended to be unmoved. The giveaways were beads of sweat popping out on his forehead and the size of his eyes.

To ease their nerves, Adolf put his hand on Quinn's head and rubbed it. Spirit Walking said something to Talking Owl. Talking Owl translated, "Spirit Walking asks if these bear dogs are from the same tribe as Yellow Grizzly."

Trying to keep from laughing, Adolf simply nodded his head. He heard Sven and Oskar chuckle behind him. Cokey, of course, didn't understand.

Adolf decided to change the subject, so he asked Talking Owl to ask Spirit Walking if the Indians would eat some elk with the white men.

The chief responded by nodding his head and rubbing his tummy.

Sven spoke up, "Ya betcha, that is a grand idea. I do have something to do the trick." He jumped up, exciting the two female dogs, and ran to the shed where he had his anvil set up. He came back grinning. He held up a steel rod with a handle on it and a couple of stands with U-shaped brackets on the top. He said, "Someone light up a roasting fire."

The Indians helped gather wood to start a fire in the fire pit. Sven set the stands on each side and Cokey helped him slid big ole slabs of elk onto the rod. They set the rod on the two brackets over the fire. Oskar ran to the bunkhouse yelling, "I will make some biscuits."

All the men, red and white, sat around the fire hungrily listening to the sizzling of dripping grease hit the fire and smelling the aroma of meat cooking in the fresh outdoor air. Before long the only sound was that of smacking as the men, and even the dogs, enjoyed the juicy elk. Adolf thought to himself, "Now, this is what Thanksgiving probably really looked like."

Chapter 38

"That's it! Sven, get your crap packed. We're going to go get the girls."
Adolf had been daydreaming most of the day - the second day of March.
Although he knew winter was far from saying goodbye, it was a nice
clear day with temperatures in the sixties. "We may get snow-bound in
the tall and uncut, but we now know it will melt again soon. You can't
help moping around, but it just ain't fair for you not to have your
sweetheart to cuddle, and I sure do miss my Caroline. We're going
tomorrow, that's it."

Sven was standing by a log he had been working on for way too long.
At first he was embarrassed by Adolf's outburst, ashamed that his
feelings were so obvious, but Adolf's words had him plumb excited. He
carefully took the broad ax to the shed, but then ran to the bunkhouse
yelling, "Ufta, just a big ole ufta! Yah-hoo! I get to go see beautiful
Neale. You betcha, I does."

Oskar had heard the shouting and came running from the whitish dun
pony he was training, "What's all the noise? Someone banged up
some?" He watched the gigantic Sven hopping around like a schoolgirl
jumping rope at recess, and looked to Adolf for an answer. He grabbed
Adolf's arm to get his attention as it seemed his other friend was
preoccupied, "Why is Sven so danged rambunctious?"

Adolf looked at Oskar and grasped him by the shoulders. "I have made
up my mind. I am taking Sven to Missouri to marry Neale and bring her
here. I'm going to go to Ohio and get Caroline also. Think you and
Cokey can take care of things here for a few months?"

Oskar reached out and hugged his longtime friend, "As friend Sven would say, ya betcha. This is something that needs to get done. It sure will be nice to eat their cooking instead of ours."

That night Adolf and Oskar were sitting on the edge of Adolf's bed with Quinn by their feet. Sven and Cokey were standing across from them exchanging insults, and Ginger and Rascal were up on Oskar's bed. The humor was on the forced side because they didn't want to be separated for months and were concerned about the dangers the trip placed on all of them. It went unspoken, but they knew it would be difficult for only two men to fight off Indian attacks or respond to an injury of some kind. Plus, all the ranch work would be resting on their shoulders. It seemed a lot to leave to the stay-at-home couple. On the other hand, traveling across Indian Territory for only two men was a concern, even if the Delaware stayed home during the winter.

Adolf cleared his voice to attract everyone's attention, "I have been doing some thinking, and think we should agree on something before Sven and I leave."

Oskar was staying so close to Adolf that he was almost sitting in his lap. After all, the two had not been without the other for many years. "What is on your mind ole buddy?"

Sven and Cokey quit messing around and sat on the bed facing the other two.

"Okay, we all understand that we are equal partners in this ranch, right?"

"Ya betcha."

"Sure enough do, Adolf."

"Darn toot'n and proud you have taken me in."

"I figure we need a name for our ranch and a brand to put on our stock," Adolf said. As the others nodded their heads, he showed them a piece of wood with just a '4' burned on it.

Puzzled looks appeared on all three of the others. Oskar asked, "A four? I don't understand. Just a four? Is there a meaning here?"

Adolf said, "Well, we are four partners and I been trying to think of something to stand for us. What you all think if we call this ranch *The Stand Alone Four?* Or we can discuss other ideas." At this point Adolf was concerned that he was out of line.

"Damn I like that," said Cokey.

Oskar punched Adolf's shoulder and yelled, "Dang ya Adolf. You're always thinking way ahead of us. I would be right proud to be known that way."

Everyone looked to Sven, because he had not said a thing. He wiped the back of his big paw across his eyes to hide some tears trying to slide down his face. "Guys, I never been part of anything before. Ya betcha, I like this and glad we did all meet up."

Although the next morning was cloudless and sunny, the atmosphere was gloomy for the four ranch owners. Adolf on Buck, with Quinn loping beside them, and Sven on Blue rode out of the valley into the start of the Great Plains and the return trip to Missouri. The grass that had been green on their arrival was a winter dead brown. It still extended as far as the eye could see, waving in reminder of how far they were from the journey's end.

"Adolf, I haves an idea that I want you to consider." Sven had stopped his blue dun just ahead of Adolf.

Adolf reined in Buck and looked at his friend, not sure where this was going. "What's on your mind, Sven?"

"It concerns the ranch. As you usually do, I been projecting to the future of the ranch. You keep telling us that this land will be all settled someday."

Adolf said, "I believe that people will continue to flow out of the east. People need land and there sure is a bunch out there." He pointed to the plains as he spoke.

Sven said, "Ya betcha, and you got me agreeing, ya surely do." He looked at Adolf and continued, "Cokey has been chatting 'bouts Texas and all the cattle herds they are rounding up."

Adolf took his hat off and scratched his head, "You do have me real confused. You seem to be jumping all around on different thoughts."

Sven shook his head and said, "No, they are all the same. Look at all this grass right here." He pointed at the grassy plain running up into the foothills.

Adolf said, "Okay. I see the grass, but so what?"

"I have been considering finding some wild cows and chasing them here as parts of our ranch. When they keep calving year after year we would have a whole bunch for when new settlers need meat." He looked a little self-conscious, worried Adolf was going to laugh at him.

Adolf looked around and said, "Sven that is a damn good idea."

Sven got excited and pointed his big hand towards the mountain range. "I've been thinking we could build another ranch house right over there for Neale and me. You all know horses and I knows cow. We still split everything four ways. That's my idea."

"And it is a damn good idea. I like it, and so will the others. We will work it out as soon as we get back."

With Sven sitting tall in his saddle, they clicked their tongues to start their horses moving and headed on the trail back to Missouri.

Chapter 39

It was cold, but not unbearable. It was the second day camping amongst the big cottonwood trees on the Smokey Hill River. Adolf and Sven had made very good time the first ten days on the trail across the Kansas Territory. They probably had gotten too comfortable with how uneventful their return trip had been going. They had seen no Indians or buffalo. There had been several short grass strips where the huge herds had harvested their share of the offerings of the Great Plains. The shortened grass in these strips was of various lengths, representing the passing time since each had been traveled.

Fuel for fire was not a problem. Thousands of buffalo chips dotted the buffalos' migration paths. Although they had no buffalo sightings, meat was still available for the taking. Elk, deer and the various species of prairie birds did not go on a winter vacation, like the buffalo seemed to have done. There were also many songbirds that were not afraid of old man winter and provided the travelers with glorious songs.

Obviously the spirits in this wild country didn't like it when mankind became too complacent. Something decided to remind the two white men why there were no Indian sightings – it was still the winter season. They woke at dawn yesterday, shivering under a blanket of damp snow. It was not just a dusting, but a six inch covering amongst the trees. Out on the prairie, a jovial wind was constantly changing where the snow should lie. Some areas had almost none; whereas, the adjoining spot may be laying claim to a wind-crusted drift. These drifts would make traveling difficult, so Adolf and Sven agreed to wait out the snow. The bright sun would make short the life of these drifts. In fact, by noon most were shrinking in size.

Unless a second storm followed the first, the travelers would be on the move tomorrow at first light.

Anxious to continue their exodus, they had prepared a quick breakfast and had the animals loaded and ready by the time dawn sprang up in the east. The early birds were waking, and created that peaceful feeling that only the chirping of birds at first light can do. Adolf took one final look at their campsite to ensure nothing was left undone. Then he re-woke Quinn, who had snuck back to bed being content to dream of whatever young dogs dream.

Impatiently Sven touched Blue's side. Neale's beautiful face was beckoning to him like the Star of Bethlehem had led the Wise Men to the cradle of Jesus centuries ago.

As they moved from the river site to the tall grass, Adolf thought of how different this trip was then all his other travels. It was quiet without his constant companion Oskar. He really missed the sound of Oskar's voice; he was used to when Oskar provided a constant background chattering, like a blue jay. The real chattering of magpies, jays, owls and whippoorwills were there, but it was not the same as Oskar's babble.

He chuckled at a couple mother killdeer who were faking broken wings and emitting pleading squeals to lead him away from their nests hidden in the grass. A large mule deer stopped her breakfast to watch the curious sight of white men slowly progressing through her land. A cute porcupine waddled off to the left on her or his early morning errand. A not so cute badger gave them the evil eye. The Great Plains were an awesome display of nature, especially at the start of day. It was not boring.

The weather held and they had covered many miles since they were delayed by the almost forgotten snowstorm ten days in the past. Again, there had been no sightings of Indians, aggressive or peaceful. But that had just changed. Off the south were eighteen riders wearing full costumes of animal skins. Several had bright colored blankets over their backs to keep them warm, and most had the center strip of hair of the Delaware.

Both Adolf and Sven had un-sheathed their rifles as they watched the hunting party. The party had also stopped, and all of the braves were watching them. A warrior with a beautiful eagle feather war bonnet led his horse a few steps toward them. He watched for a few heartbeats, then raised his war lance over his head and slowly lowered it to the back of his horse. His right hand rose to the height of his shoulder before turning palm outward in the sign of peace.

Watching the Indians' movements, Adolf recognized Spotted Elk – the leader of the war party they had defeated on their first trip. Adolf quickly raised his own hand, palm out, as the two respectfully gazed at each other. Someone must have taught Spotted Elk some English words, because the words 'Kill-From-Afar' drifted to Adolf's ears. Spotted Elk turned his horse west and the band followed him.

Sven said, "Ufta that was sure something. I never thought I would ever see that. It ran a tingle down my back."

Adolf just sat there watching the Indian warriors. Although he didn't say anything, he was overwhelmed. Maybe the Indians had something in their belief of a spirit world. He surprisingly felt a warm closeness between him and Spotted Elk, even though they were adversaries.

Nothing unusual happened during the remainder of the trip and they were glad it was coming to its fruition. Adolf and Oskar were sitting at the opening to the Slash N ranch feeling like they were home. The two barns with corrals were to the left and the sprawling ranch house was on the right. Uncle Gottlieb was heading for the house. Aunt Ailish was waiting for him a couple steps from the front porch. Some movement must have caught her eye because she turned to look at the ranch entrance, using her hand to shade her eyes. Adolf waved his hat and, after a short pause, his aunt started bouncing up and down. She waved with her left hand and pointed with her right to direct her husband to the travelers. She started to run toward the boys and her shouts reached their ears, "They're back. Gottlieb, the boys are back!"

In a few long strides, Adolf's uncle had caught up with his excited wife. They stood arm in arm, waving at Adolf and Oskar. Running from the barn was Neale; she was made obvious by the raven black hair streaming behind her when she threw her hat in the air.

Sven kicked Blue into a gallop toward his betrothed, and reached a gigantic arm around her waist to pull her up on his gray dun. She wrapped her arms around Sven's neck, knocking his hat to the ground unintentionally.

Adolf had mixed emotions as he watched his cousin and his friend. He was happy for them, but also felt sadness wash over him as he was

214

missing his own betrothed – Caroline. She was still so far away in Ohio. He remembered his aunt and uncle waiting for him, so he pulled his eyes back to them and walked Buck forward. He reined up beside them as Uncle Gottlieb shouted, "Welcome back. Damn nice to see you."

As Adolf dismounted, his aunt threw her arms around him and said, "We have the best surprise in the world for you, dear Adolf."

Adolf held her at arm's length trying to decipher what she was saying. Over her head, something in his line of vision tugged his eyes to the north of the house; there was white canvas flapping in the breeze. A large prairie schooner was sitting under the oak grove with a middle-aged couple standing by the front wheel. Before he had time for this to register his eyes moved toward someone running at him and shouting his name, over and over. It was Caroline, but she was in Ohio, wasn't she?

The voice of Aunt Ailish brought him out of his trance, "Go to her dear boy."

Quinn thought this was a new game and barked happily as he raced Adolf toward his love. Adolf, the young man who always was reserved, erupted as he grabbed Caroline in his arms saying over and over – "I love you, I love you, I love you."

His head was full of her laughter and then her words, "I love you too."

Chapter 40

The Adam's covered wagon stood forty feet from the gravesites of Milton and Luther. There was a large campfire blazing away. Adolf was engrossed in a letter his parents had sent with Caroline. It was explaining what had happened in Ohio. Mr. Caldwell Coulter tried to make life tough for Adolf's parents by telling people in the town of Jackson, Ohio to boycott Olaf and Belinda's ranch. Mr. Nagel said he got a kick out of that because none of his customers lived in Jackson. But, since Paul Adam's gunsmith shop was in Jackson, the boycott did cost him business.

The Adams family decided the hell with it, and decided to bring Caroline out West. They sold the shop at a good price. They also sold the small ranch at a profit, so had the funds to open a business somewhere else. They decided that would be somewhere in the west.

Adolf's aunt and uncle had joined Adolf sitting around the warming fire with the Adams family. Gottlieb said, "We really don't have any towns close by and the Ambler's trading post gets most of the gun business around here."

Adolf was only half listening to the conversation, but he put the letter down and looked over to his future in-laws. "I don't know how soon they are going to start settling in the Kansas Territory, but they will someday." He thought some more and added, "You know what? There are some businesses starting to open around Fort John. A sawmill is now open. There are signs that a town will spring up someday in the near future."

Paul looked at his wife Mary with a 'what if' look, "What are your thoughts?"

Caroline's mom took ahold of her daughter's hand, "It would be nice to stay close to the kids. Think of having grandkids to spoil."

Paul smiled as he said, "That would be nice. We don't have anything holding us back. I think it is worth a try. Nothing ventured, nothing gained."

Mary looked at Adolf and Caroline and, with a quiver in her voice, said, "What about you two? Would we be invading your space?"

Caroline looked at Adolf, "It would be nice to have family close by. Don't you think, Adolf?"

"I sure wouldn't have suggested it if I thought it would be an inconvenience. You can stay at the ranch until you get settled in someplace." Then he chuckled, "As my friend Sven says, there is plenty of room in our valley for all the families. We also have a second valley that's even larger."

Ailish spoke up, "Oh, how wonderful for you all."

Sven and Neale came walking from the barn arm in arm. Neale asked, "What's wonderful?"

Later, Adolf and Caroline were beyond the corrals, strolling amongst the large herd of Fox Trotters. Several types of sparrows took turns practicing landings and take offs. Male black and white lark buntings, with their more conservative mates, sprang up ahead of the walkers. The loud thumping of a pileated woodpecker searching for bugs in some dead tree could be heard from the nearby forest. The presence of a skunk could be smelled, but not seen. The grazing horses were sharing the brown grass with five gray mule deer, who popped their heads up to see if the man and women were a threat.

"Caroline, I have never said it out loud, but I want you to be my wife." Adolf stopped and faced her, "Will you marry me before we head across the territories?"

"Oh yes! That is what I want to do. I never want to be without you again."

"I know Sven and Neale are planning to wed before we start our trek. Maybe we can make it a double wedding."

Caroline tossed her dark brown hair and chuckled, "Neale and I have it all planned out all ready." She pulled Adolf to her, "Your uncle has arranged for a minister to be here Sunday for the ceremony. Hope you don't mind my presumption."

"I don't mind. I didn't know how to make it happen, but it makes my heart fill with happiness."

The little country church was overflowing with well-wishers. Most were long time neighbors and friends of the Nagel family, including the Triple D owners, the Dvork brothers and their families. Of course the Slash N ranch hands were present, including Shorty, Timmy, and Slim in their Sunday best, along with three new hands.

A very proud Uncle Gottlieb walked his daughter down the aisle. Her raven-black hair was a gorgeous contrast to her ivory wedding dress, which was her mother Ailish's. Walking beside them was an equally proud Mr. Adams with his daughter Caroline on his arm. She was equally ravishing in her own mother's snowy white dress. The hair of both brides was adorned with artificially made flowers: white forget-me-nots for Neale and yellow daisies for Caroline.

After the vows were taken the minister presented the new couples, Mr. and Mrs. Nelson and Mr. and Mrs. Nagel, to the cheering attendees. All of the women had contributed a special food dish for the celebration. Several of the men had brought their musical instruments, and a polka hoedown sprang to life.

The next day Slim shyly approached Adolf, "May I ask you a question?"

Adolf tore his thoughts away from his new wife for a moment when he realized how serious Slim was acting. He stood up from the overturned bucket he had been sitting on and nodded to Slim.

"I do like it here at the Slash N, but I miss the mustang horses. Could I possibly go to work for you guys on your new ranch?" He nervously wrung his hands together before looking down and kicking his scuffed boots in the dirt.

Adolf considered the question. Hiring ranch hands was nothing he had thought about, but knew it would need to happen someday. "We are just building and can't pay wages yet," cautioned Adolf.

"I don't need wages now. I can wait until you can afford them."

"Let me talk to Sven, but I think the answer will be yes. The herd is growing and we can pay you something when we sell some of the green broke ponies." Adolf looked at Slim to see his reaction.

Slim had a smile on his face as he said, "I reckon that is fair."

As Slim walked away, Adolf thought that it would be good to have another gun traveling across the wide open prairie. Slim's knowledge of cattle horses would come in handy and, after all, he was the man who had planted the seed in Adolf's mind.

Adolf saw Mr. Adams rearranging something in the covered wagon, so he walked over to give him a hand. Adolf was surprised with the contents of the schooner. He expected to see a garbled mess of household furniture. Instead, it was neatly packed with Paul's inventory from his gun shop. Adolf asked, "Where's your furniture?"

"We sold most with the house," Paul said with a smile. "The missus and I figured we could not haul both our inventory and furniture across the whole country. The Bartholomew family bought most of it with the house."

Adolf looked over the inventory, "I've been meaning to discuss something with you."

Mr. Adams stopped fussing with the load to pay attention to Adolf. "And what is that?"

"I sure love the Paterson pistols, but they have a huge flaw."

"Oh. What is that? I find them to be very accurate, and they are the only pistol with more than one shot."

"We've been damn lucky in our altercations with Indians. In a heated battle there ain't enough time to reload. You virtually have to take the darn gun totally apart to put in powder, lead and, then caps. There has to be some way to fix the pistols to load faster. Do you have any ideas?"

Mr. Adams nodded his head, "You ain't the first to complain. The Colt Company has had a lot of complaints regarding the gun's reloading. Young Samuel has announced they are working on an improved gun, they hope to market it by 1839."

Adolf frowned, "Well that sure doesn't help us right now. Those Indians aren't going to hold off attacking until then."

Mr. Adams slapped Adolf's arm as he laughed, "Your point is well taken. Colt made additional cylinders as a short term solution. I brought a bunch with me; I was planning to surprise you with them."

Adolf uttered, "Good. And thanks"

"In the meantime, I have come up with my own alteration. I can jerry-rig the pistols by changing the arbor so the cylinder and breach can be quickly popped out and new ones inserted rapidly."

"Damn! That sounds like a fantastic thing. Will this fix take long?"

"No Adolf, it will only take a couple hours. But better yet, I brought along some that I have already altered. I will trade them out with each of you."

"Damn, Mr. Adams. I take my hat off to you. I do believe that you are the first person to ever solve my problem before I identified it. Thank you."

Mr. Adam slapped his knee and snorted a sound of contentment at the praise. "My pleasure, young man."

Mr. Adams opened a couple of boxes to show Adolf another item. He explained that a lot of his customers didn't return to recover guns they had left him to repair. Therefore, he had several unclaimed guns, mostly 12 gauge or 16 gauge shotguns.

At Adolf's suggestion, he provided shotguns to those that didn't have one; which included his wife and daughter, as well as Sven and Slim. Neale had her own double barrel 12 gauge tucked into a scabbard by her left leg as well, as a Colt Paterson she had obtained from Mr. Adams.

Adolf and Mr. Adams finished rearranging the wagon, so Neale's bed room set and clothes could be loaded. But Adolf's thoughts were on their upcoming trip—any Indians that attacked this little group was in for one heck of a surprise.

Chapter 41

Like the previous send off, Uncle Gottlieb's family and ranch crew were standing in the front yard waving goodbye to the westward travelers. There was one major difference – Neale was not in the waving group. She was riding a red Fox Trotter gelding, that she called Foxy, alongside Sven on Blue. Tears were rolling down her face in an uncontrolled display of emotion. She was sad leaving the family she had lived with her whole life, but they were also tears of joy; she was riding beside her husband into the land of their future.

Caroline was mounted on Betsy, her black Tennessee Walker, and she rode beside Adolf. Quinn was trotting on the heels of Buck, although he was much larger than when he was a puppy. He was almost full grown, standing over three feet at the shoulders, and when his front paws were standing on Adolf's shoulders he had to look down at Adolf's eyes.

They were leading. Paul and Mary Adams were following, perched on the seat of their large prairie schooner pulled by six strong Belgium draft horses and leading two saddlers. Adolf's dad Olaf had arranged for the Adams to obtain a discount on horses from Adolf's grandfather.

Slim was bringing up the rear aboard his fawn dun mustang, with Adolf's mule on a lead.

"Sven, I am going to miss mom, dad, and my brothers." Neale was straining to see her family as the procession rounded the first curve in the entryway.

Sven reached over to grasp her hand, "I know you will. That never goes away. I still miss my family and know I always will, but sure helps knowing you are with me." He displayed a grin that would have been too large for any other face and said, "You're going to love the Stand Alone 4. It is almost as beautiful as you."

Neale stopped her roan and stared back in the direction of the Slash N ranch; Sven patiently sat and watched her from his saddle. Then she turned Foxy and trotted after the covered wagons, "Come on, big guy. Let's go build our house."

"What a disappointment." Sven had been telling Neale how awesome the first sight of the Great Plains was going to be, but the first sight was nothing like he remembered. "Adolf, this is sure the wrong picture."

Adolf was gazing out onto the prairie as he said, "I don't remember this a few weeks ago. I think we were not very observant last trip."

They both remembered that the grass was a winter brown instead of the lush green of their first trip, but that was the least of the difference. The heavy weight of drifted snow had packed much of the grassland flat and broken lots of dried grass stems. There were large patches of the tall grassland, but not the overwhelming constant five feet grass that they had originally stopped to comment about. This compounded the disappointment that the new travelers felt, because they knew the large herds of buffalo were probably still on their southern migration.

"What's wrong?" Caroline asked as she reached out for Adolf's arm.

"I just expected it to be more like our first trip. We wanted to see the awe in your eyes when you first looked over tall prairie grass from here to the far horizon,"

Adolf had everyone gather around. "I think time and water are going to be our worst enemies. We need to cross all the rivers before they flood from the mountain snow runoff. The wagon slows us down, so I think we have another five or six weeks to go."

"What about the savages?" Mr. Adams was looking out over the prairie as if he expected to see thousands of Indians riding across the grassland, similar to the stories of the Mongolian hoards in Asia Minor.

"First, not all the Indians are aggressive. Second, I hope most have migrated south for the winter with the buffalo. We'll see some, but mostly they will be hunting not on some rampage."

"What if you are mistaken?" Paul responded.

Adolf looked at Paul, "Then I hope we are armed well enough to discourage any attacks."

They had made it past the Smoky Hill River and were almost to the Republican River. The Smoky Hill River had been flowing well beyond its normal channel but had still been passable. April showers had brought rain, and even hail, to the region, and the new grass was greening the land. Where the buffalo had eaten, the grass was already up six to eight inches. Slim wondered if a family of fairies were planting seed during the night or just throwing out fairy dust.

Luck regarding Indians had also favored the travelers. They had seen isolated groups, but none had made an effort to attack. Maybe that luck was about to change. A small group of riders had been parallel to them for the past hour and did not seem to be moving away. They had disappeared behind a ridge south of them and not reappeared yet. Adolf was nervous and it was evident the others were also. All had weapons drawn, and Paul Adams couldn't keep his eyes away from the ridge. He looked as if even a mouse had charged over the hill, he would declare war.

As they approached the other end of the ridge, they saw the group of warriors waiting for them atop brown and white pinto horses. Both horses and Indians were decorated with feathers and colorful paint.

"Indians!" screamed Mr. Adams, and Mrs. Adams expelled a surprised shriek.

Adam turned around in the saddle as fast as he could yell, "Don't shoot, Mr. Adams." He was afraid his words would have no effect, but he saw Sven reach up and pull the shotgun away from Mr. Adams.

Paul Adams tried to retrieve the gun as he yelled, "Shoot the heathens."

Sven spoke loudly to get through to Mr. Adams, "Calm down. They are friendly." He then yelled back to Slim who also had a gun out, "You too Slim. These are tame Injuns."

Adam saw that Sven had the situation under control, so he turned back to Spirit Walking and his band and yelled, "My friend Spirit Walking. It pleases my heart to see you have hair."

227

Talking Owl was beside his chief and repeated Adolf's words. This changed the look of surprise Spirit Walking was showing at Mr. Adams initial action to a beaming smile. His smooth voice yelled words of the Cheyenne. Talking Owl translated, "He says the spirits are shining on the people to bring his brother Na-gel onto the hunting ground of the Cheyenne."

Adolf rode to the Indians and he and Spirit Walking grasped arms to show the bond of brothers. Adolf had all his companions come forward to meet the Indians. He told them, "This is my brother Spirit Walking, a much powerful chief of the great Cheyenne people."

Spirit Walking beamed when this was translated. After being introduced, Talking Owl translated his words, "He is proud to meet the tribe of Kills-From-Afar. He and Yellow Grizzly have chosen their wives wisely and he prays the Great Spirit honors them with many sons."

As they watched the band of Indians riding towards the south, Caroline commented, "Now there is a real statesman. What a majestic picture they make. They really represent the beauty of these Great Plains."

Neale added her comments, "Wow. You got that right, Caroline. Spirit Walking's bearing sent chills down my spine. I never understood the real meaning of Indian before."

Paul Adams spoke up, "What a fool I was to call them savages. That Spirit Walker is impressive. Very impressive. I would be tempted to vote for him if he ran for any public office."

Mary Adams was standing with a look of disbelief and turned to her son-in-law, "Adolf, I have to admit meeting your friends is a true highlight for my life. I would never believe in a thousand years how much I misunderstood those people."

The following dawn they rode through a shower of snow pelting them like blowing sand and stinging their skin just as much. None wanted to stop so they wrapped scarves over their faces and leaned into the wind. By mid-day the sun had evaporated the clouds and provided much appreciated warmth. No sign existed that the snow was anything except their imagination. They found the Republican River swollen and overflowing its main channel. Adolf rode Buck across the now wide river to test its depth. The fast moving water was over his stirrups and got his boots and pants wet. The swift current provided Adolf concern as to getting the heavily loaded covered wagon safely across.

Adolf re-crossed to rejoin the others on the bank and discuss getting everyone and the wagon across. They sure didn't want to lose Mr. Adams valuable cargo. Even more of concern was that they didn't want to lose a life.

Mary got off the wagon seat and mounted her black mare. Then Adolf led all three women across and returned a second time to help with the prairie schooner. The men tied ropes to the up-river side of the wagon and attached the other end to their mounts as well as to the mule and Paul's horse. They surmised that this would keep the schooner from being swept downstream. Sven lifted Quinn and put him beside Mr. Adams on the wagon seat. Quinn started to whine and plead with Adolf to come get him. Adolf put his palm out and said, "Stay!" The big dog didn't like that, but he lay down and panted like a steam engine.

All let out a breath of relief when the wagon rolled out of the river like a huge prehistoric dinosaur, water slewing from its underside. The six monstrous Belgium draft horses were straining forward to tug the schooner through the deep mud, Quinn barking encouragement all the way up the bank.

"Now that was downright fearsome," Caroline's father said as he pulled out a rumpled bandana to wipe sweat from his brow. "Let's hope we don't have to do that again."

Sven received a dirty look when he rode his stallion to the wagon to pat Paul on the leg and said, "You done me proud old timer." It wasn't the proud part that bothered the elder man. Catching the evil eye directed at him, Sven let out a chuckle, "Did ja wet your bloomers?"

"I sure didn't so leave me alone before I come down and take a switch to your backside you oversized oaf." He burst out laughing as he added, "I did come mighty close to staining my drawers though."

When Sven lifted Quinn down, the wolfhound made a point of rushing over to water a tree, causing the whole group to explode with merriment.

"If you help me off this seat I think I will join Quinn for some much needed relief," joked Mr. Adams. This humorous exchange helped to expel the tension for everyone.

Adolf suggested they take their lunch break. They led the animals to some nice tender green grass before eating a nice meal set out by the women.

"Much better than our own cooking ain't it Adolf?" Sven squeezed out between bites of a humungous venison sandwich made with trail-made bread.

Adolf started to give his friend a sour look, but smiled instead and said, "You got that right. Now let me eat my lunch or I'll help Mr. Adams give you that much needed spanking."

Sven almost fell over backward with the image of Adolf and Paul trying to wrestle him over someone's knee.

Slim put aside his bashfulness and said, "I would pay good coin to see that, I surely would."

After a short rest filled with casual conversation, they hitched the Belgians and headed toward the Rocky Mountains. Adolf decided that this last experience had truly bonded the group. He was comfortable with this extended family.

Adolf stopped the group to point out that the Rocky Mountains were visible on the horizon. "We're getting close. We'll be there in a couple days."

Sven said, "Wait till you sees the valley. It'll take your breath away, you betcha it will."

Although time seemed to stand still, the new arrivals were gawking and expressing laudations the closer they came to the Rocky Mountains. Then, to their surprise, they were looking out over the Stand Alone Four.

Caroline was the first to speak, "Unbelievable! Why it is more breath taking than I could ever imagine."

Mary said, "You are right Caroline. I don't think I have ever seen a setting so picturesque."

Caroline leaned from her horse to kiss Adolf on the cheek. "Sweetheart, this is perfect. Thank you husband, and you too, Sven."

"My golly! Look at all them horses," Slim uttered as his eyes took in the sight. "I never figured you all would have so many already. Damn! Oh, pardon me ladies. My mouth done outrun my brain."

"Welcome home," Adolf said as he sat proudly in front of his little troop.

He was interrupted from saying more by the loud clanging of a triangle, which Cokey was banging. Oskar was jumping up and down and waving his hat as his red hair blew in the wind. Ginger and Rascal joined the greeting by barking excitably and running circles around the yard. It was a good reunion.

Chapter 42

Finally, after two weeks of backbreaking work, the six men had completed the ranch house. It was a good sized house, thirty two feet wide and thirty six feet deep, with a smaller ten by twelve back mudroom. The north side consisted of a large eighteen by eighteen foot kitchen at the front and a same size parlor behind it. The north kitchen wall mainly consisted of a huge natural stone fireplace and one door. Sven had built in various cooking surfaces including an enclosed baking oven. A smaller fireplace had been built in the parlor, also on the north side, to maximize the effect of heat in the winter. Mrs. Adams helped design cabinetry in the kitchen to hold food, utensils, and firewood, along with large surfaces to prepare food.

The left side of the house incorporated three large bedrooms with shelving to place clothing and extra bedding. All three were covered by a low ceiling to keep heat in. A large sleeping loft had been constructed over the kitchen. It had been separated to make two sleeping areas with space for children to play. Although the upper wall toward the parlor went from the floor to the ceiling, the inside end of both were open to allow kitchen heat to warm the areas.

All the outer walls were eighteen inches thick. Green willow sticks had been twisted and shoved between the cracks before both the outside and inside were plastered with adobe. The window openings all were built with defense in mind. At Adolf's instructions thick wooden window inserts had been built to open inwards. Each contained two firing slits three inches wide. One extending from bottom to top and the other side to side, crossing in the middle. They were hinged on the inside to pull open in the warm weather. The thick walls allowed for a large shelf to place ammunition when fighting. Each window also had a thick wooden, inner insert to help keep the cold out during winter.

The mudroom had shelves for boots and pegs for coats.

All six men and three women were standing in front of the finished house admiring their construction. Neale said, "It is gorgeous. With the aspen trees in back and the mountains above, the setting is perfect. Don't you think, Caroline?"

"Yes I do. The spring outside the kitchen door will be handy too."

Mrs. Adams spoke up, "I am envious of you young women. Think of all the years you will have to enjoy this place. I am very happy for all of you."

It had been decided that the Adams would share the cabin with the other married couples until they relocated to their final destination.

Mr. Adams finally broke up the viewing, "Well, let's get everyone moved in."

The moving was done and all nine were sitting around the kitchen table. Slim had built the long table and a dozen chairs. All nine were enjoying an after dinner toast. Adolf stood up holding his glass, "First I want to thank everyone for their efforts and also thank these three beautiful women for a very tasty meal."

The other men raised their glasses in salute, while the women bowed their heads.

"I would also like to toast our first meal in this wonderful house, no, make that home. Mr. Adams may I call upon you to say a prayer to the Lord in thanks for what we have?"

"Son, and that is meant to express my acceptance of you as the husband to my daughter, I would be much honored to say a blessing." He stood up and asked everyone to join hands. Bowing his head he prayed:

"Our Father in Heaven, thank you for providing this beautiful blessing you have bestowed on all these young people. Thank you for looking over them and I pray you continue to watch over these wonderful people as they start out life in this land of Eden that you have led them to. Please guide them in their pursuit of a new start in this land of opportunity. Bless them in family, as that is the most profound goal any of us can hope to endeavor to obtain as followers of your word. May peace and love follow these wonderful people throughout their lives and the lives of their children. I want to also thank you for allowing my wife and me to be part of this family and to share in this experience. In your name, Amen."

Later that night they were all brought out of their peaceful dreams by loud rumbling to the west, reminding them of Norse legends of Thor's mighty hammer. The thunder was joined by bolts of lightning, as if Odin had declared war against some lesser Norse god; the flashing erased the darkness of the night and replaced it with light.

Rain started pounding the roof as if some giant was executing a perfect continuation of a multi-beat drum roll. The six married people left their beds to peer out the windows. They could see the three single men looking out of the bunkhouse door. The rain was not just flowing off the roof, it was flying off in large torrents, gushing onto the meadow and hurrying back toward the Cache la Poudre River.

All other sound was suddenly overwhelmed by a rumble many times louder than the thunder. It was the sound of nightmares, and it was increasing in volume as it advanced from the west. All eyes were glued to where the river entered on the west end of the property. Like the sudden eruption of a volcano, a fifteen foot wall of water charged down the river carrying trees, animal carcasses, and anything caught in its path. The roar was so loud it hurt their ears and cause all three dogs to cower in corners and whine in uncontrollable fear. All the animals in the corrals were bucking in fear and trying to bust through the rails on the south side, away from the river. It was evident they were screaming, but no sound could be heard above the mighty roar of the flooding river.

Adolf was trying to appear calm, but felt as panicked as all the others. How high would the river rise? He held his breath, watching the fence disappear under the water as the river overflowed its banks. He knew the land rose from the river toward the mountains, but how many feet was the change in elevation?

Caroline was in his arms and her eyes were as big as dinner plates. She was looking to Adolf for protection as she asked, "Are we safe here or is the river going to get this high?"

Adolf was silent, not because of his nature, but because he had no answer.

Mr. Adams, looking as scared as his daughter, peered out the window, "Surely it won't reach this high." But his voice quivered in uncertainty.

As quick as it had erupted, the sound fell away as the worst of the water wall flew out of the valley. The advancing river started returning to the river a good quarter mile from the buildings. Adolf was thanking the Lord that they had chosen to build on the south side instead of toward the river. He wished that is was his knowledge that had made the choice, but he knew that was not the case. It was just dumb luck.

The next morning the men gathered together by the corral to discuss the plan for the day. Although the ground was wet, the main evidence of the flood was the debris covering the flood plain. The mess included full-sized trees, broken branches, waterlogged brush, and bloating bodies of deer, rabbits, a skunk, two bears and a unfortunate pinto mustang. They had just finished tossing them back into the Cache to let it carry the dead to the South Platt.

Adolf leaned on the top rail, "We need to gather more mustangs and we need to start raising the barn"

Paul spoke up, "I should go to that fort you mentioned to see about opening a gun shop." He cast his eyes down and his face turned red. He didn't want to put the others out.

Sven said, "By golly, sure crave to start the barn. Not that we don't need more stock, but I am really anxious to see that barn sitting there. I really am."

Adolf said, "We may be able to accomplish two missions at the same time. We don't have near enough wood for the barn and our order is sitting at the mill by Fort John. Mr. Adams could drive a wagon to the fort and see about his needs while we pick up more wood." He placed a foot on the bottom rail and rested his chin on the top rail.

Oskar wanted to support his best friend, "Good idea, Adolf. If we start on the barn then next week, some of us can round up horses while some are working on the barn." He backed up to the corral and hooked his elbows over the top rail next to Adolf.

Cokey said, "I ain't had no beer for a gosh dang long time and I is sure hankering for one. I am volunteering myself for the fort trip." He smiled at the others to ensure they knew he would go with whatever the decision was.

"Guys, I ain't got any druthers. Whatever you decide, I am honored to pitch in," Slim looked up from where he was drawing circles in the mud. "Of course I am nighty anxious to see those herds of wild mustangs. Never seen that before."

Adolf looked over to Paul and asked, "If we make a trip to the fort, do you reckon we can haul back lumber in your schooner?"

Paul grinned at Adolf, "Damn tooting we can. Especially if that is the deciding factor for going or not." Then he chuckled.

Adolf said, "How about I go with Mr. Adams to the fort and see if all our lumber needs are waiting for us. We can take two wagons and get enough lumber to have a nice start on the barn." He glanced around the group and asked, "Does this sound right for everyone?"

He got nods from everyone, but saw the downturned mouth of Cokey. He decided to let Cokey dangle for a couple more minutes, "Okay, that's what we will do. Paul, let's hook up your horses."

As he and Mr. Adams started into corral to get the big Belgians, Cokey hesitated for a few heartbeats, and then started following Sven toward the mustangs they were going to work with.

"Damn it Cokey, I damn well ain't planning to hitch the mules to your wagon, so get over here pronto and do it yourself or you ain't coming along."

The loud explosion of laughter brought all three women out of the house and caused the dogs to bark. Meanwhile, Cokey was left standing there with his mouth wide open.

Sven punched Cokey in the arm and sent him in a scramble forward. "Hey pint size, drink a mug for me." He dug his hand into his pocket and tossed Cokey a dime. "Have a couple on me old timer." Then he cackled all the way to the horses.

Cocky caught up with Adolf and Paul and said, "That was a damn mean trick Adolf." He smiled real big and added, "You did catch me with my pants down, yes you did."

Adolf threw his arm around Cokey's shoulders, "Darn near thought you broke your jaw when it hit the ground."

Cokey started giggling and Mr. Adams smiled at the two young men. He said, "I sure do enjoy the way you all get along. It is a pleasure to behold."

Chapter 43

Adolf was amazed by the changes he saw around Fort John. The Indian encampment was basically the same, maybe a little larger, but lots of changes had occurred regarding the white man. In addition to the trading post and the lumber mill, several wooden buildings had been added, along with various sized tents. A small settlement was in the midst of being established. The time for Mr. Adams to open his gun shop was definitely now.

"Wow-zee, look at all them new saloons sprouted up?" Cokey exclaimed as he snapped the reins on the backs of the mules and directed them towards the sawmill. "A thirsty man has got all kinds of choices to cure his thirst."

Mr. Adams was too busy gawking to respond. And of course Cokey's comment was not something that Adolf felt needed a reply.

As they pulled up to the mill they saw huge piles of sawed lumber covered by canvas. A gray-bearded gent in homespun covered with saw dust glanced at them and smiled when he recognized Adolf. Walking toward them with his hand stuck out, his gravelly voice stated, "Mr. Nagel, if memory serves me right. Betcha you is coming for your lumber."

Adolf climbed off Buck and petted the big head of Quinn who had startled the owner of the mill. He then grabbed Perk Perkins's hand to shake as well as to keep him from running from Quinn. "At least what we can haul in the two wagons."

After being pointed to their canvas covered planks, Adolf said to Mr. Adams, "Perk is sending over a couple of his men to help load. If it is alright with you two, I need to talk to the major. Go ahead and load what you can. I'll be back shortly."

Cocky laughed as he said, "Go ahead Adolf, we don't need you. Figured you would skip out on the work anyways, I surely did."

Adolf grinned as he mounted Buck and told Quinn to stay. Arriving at the major's, he was surprised to see that the headquarters tent had been replaced with an adobe building. Things were starting to grow up fast in the territory.

Major Hitchcock was downright pleased to see Adolf. He grasped Adolf's hand with both of his, and dang near pumped it plumb off. "What a sight for these eyes. Your visits are always a pleasure. I heard you went after your lady friend, so I assume you brought her back."

Adolf grinned in response.

After casual conversation, the army officer asked, "What can I do for you?"

"I just thought I should verify if you still need horses."

"Actually we have pretty much all we need right now, but the commander for the new stockade just north of here, Fort Platte, said to tell you they need about three hundred and will pay the same $15 a head."

Adolf almost choked when he calculated that this would be $4,500, damn near a fortune. "We have 150 ready today and can have the rest ready in a couple months.

Major Hitchcock smiled, "Pretty much as I figured. I told the commander of the fort I would let him know for sure. I'll send a rider tomorrow and have them send wranglers to your ranch to pick up the ones you got and pay you at the same time."

"That sounds good. We'll be ready for them." Adolf sat back and, to be polite, asked, "How's things going for you?"

The major frowned, sat back in his chair, and slammed a fist on his desk. "We got some problems. Some skunks are causing problem with the trappers and even with some of those new businesses outside the fort."

Adolf leaned forward with interest, "This is surprising news. Guess growth always brings all kinds of people."

Major Hitchcock's shoulders sagged with despair, "You're right, but I wasn't expecting this. We have had nine trappers killed. The bastards tried to fool us into blaming the Indians. The killed were all scalped and arrows were scattered about. Whoever it is, they are downright stupid. The arrows were a mixture of Ute, Pawnee, and Arapaho. Who is dumb enough to believe those tribes would bind together? Even dumber, they had added arrows with wood that was not hardened and the feathers were a mixture of quail, duck, and geese. Have you ever known an Indian to use different types of feathers on a single arrow?"

A slight huff escaped from Adolf as he considered how anyone could be so ignorant. "That is just plain ludicrous."

"The Sargent Major was so exasperated he near exploded. He had a couple Indian scouts with him and they burst out laughing at the crude attempts to make the fake arrows. The arrow points were not even sharp enough to cut butter."

"Who do reckon is behind this?"

"Of course all the dead trappers' furs were stolen, but they also took their weapons, moccasins, and food. I can see Indians taking guns, but not white men's footwear or food. Only another white man would do that."

Adolf leaned back and crossed his arms, "You are right about that. These criminals are white men."

"I have posted a bounty of $20 per outlaw, dead or alive. No matter to me. I just want it to stop."

Adolf found the wagons about half loaded when he got back to the mill, so he joined in to help. After they were done, Adolf told Paul and Cokey about his two discussions with Major Hitchcock. Both came as a shock to the other two men.

"It makes me somewhat nervous about opening a store with that going on," Mr. Adams remarked. "Still, I will drive the schooner over to the trading post and talk to the owner."

Adolf said, "You can join up with Cokey and me at that saloon with the red sign. We are going to stop there to let him have his dang beer."

Cocky was smiling ear to ear and rubbing his hands together, "It's sure thoughtful of you, young Adolf."

At the saloon, Adolf had Quinn stay with the wagon as he followed his smaller friend into the smoke filled bar. Although only a few months old the saloon already smelled of stale beer, man stink, and wet sawdust. To their surprise, the glasses were clean and the beer cold. The bartender, a clean shaven man wearing a brown derby and red suspenders that held up his wool trousers over a clean white shirt, told them that they had stored ice off the lakes in sawdust. Most of the ice had melted, but he figured they had enough to last another week. He took their dime and tossed it into a cigar box.

The two men took their mugs over to a table and settled into a delightful conversation. Both were excited about the prospect of making so much money. Adolf toasted Cocky, "My friend, you have proven to be a wonderful partner. Without you this dream may not have come true. I toast you for our prosperity."

Cocky was not used to such praise, especially from someone he held in such high esteem. He blushed bright red before tapping his mug against Adolf's. "Adolf, this past year has been the highpoint of my life. I am thankful to that wrangler up above for bringing you three partners into this humble cowboy's life."

Just at that moment they heard angry barking and a loud voice outside, "I said get away from him." Loud angry barking was followed by the explosion of a gun being fired. Adolf took off for the door so fast that his chair flew backward to slam against a trapper walking behind it. Cocky took his mug with him as he followed.

Their lumber filled wagon was surrounded by men in buckskin, all armed. At first Adolf didn't recognize any faces, than he saw Crazy Jake standing with his back to a very agitated Quinn. Saliva was dripping from the dog's open mouth and his lips were drawn back to provide full benefit to the size of his fangs. Crazy Jake held a flintlock pistol in each hand, one with smoke drifting from its barrel. He was snarling almost as much as Quinn.

Another known face was standing facing Jake with his rifle pointed in Jake and Quinn's direction - the swine Gumbo Pete. Standing behind Gumbo were eight other men as disgusting looking as he. They were all pointing weapons in the same direction as Gumbo, but were standing very nervously, because they were surrounded by fourteen trappers armed to the teeth.

"Crazy Jake, what's going on here?" Adolf's voice froze everyone as if they were turned to pillars of salt. The click of the hammer cocking on his Colt Paterson pierced the tense air. A second click sounded when Cokey cocked his pistol.

Without turning his gaze away from Gumbo Pete, Crazy Jake yelled, "Your monster dog surprised these gents when they tried to steal your wagon." His voice rose as he said, "The polecats decided to shoot your hero dog, but I wasn't havin' any of that chicken shit behavior."

"We weren't stealing the lumber, just lookin', when this wild animal attacked us. Figured it was our duty to blast him to Kingdom Come; keep it from eating innocent children. Crazy Jake is just plumb crazy he is." He looked around and said, "Would have got the job done if his friends wouldn't have ganged up on us."

He looked at Adolf and recognition spread across his face. He started to tremble, "It is just a misunderstanding. That's what it is. Let's go boys." His band lowered their guns and slunk off as fast as their legs would allow.

Adolf holstered his pistol and looked hard at Crazy Jake, "I believe I owe you and your friends a beer. What do you say?"

"Sounds damn friendly-like." Jake looked at Quinn and said, "Golly! That pup sure gots big and a real powerful watchdog he is." Then he looked at the lumber, "I don't trust them varmints from sneaking back."

A tall, balding trapper with his left ear gone stepped forward, "Sam and I don't drink anymore. We can stay watch-out and it would be a pleasure. Ain't you those gents living down on the Cache?"

Adolf answered, "Yes we are. I am thankful for your offer." He put an arm around Crazy Jake and Cokey as he led them back into the bar. He turned his head to whistle for Quinn to follow. He wasn't going to risk his four-legged friend again.

As he sat down, he thought about what had just happened and wondered if they had met Major Hitchcock's new problem.

Chapter 44

The wagon Cokey drove was leading them south toward the Stand Alone Four ranch. Adolf was riding beside him, with Quinn trailing. The Irish wolfhound was still remembering the big chunk of bear meat the bartender had tossed to him.

Mr. Adams and the large schooner were following. Paul was whistling a tune, unrecognizable due to his lack of any musical talent. He yanked the big draft horses to a stop when Quinn growled deeply and started forward with stiff legs. The hound's wire-like hair was standing straight up, like the hairstyle of the Delaware braves that rode with Spotted Elk.

Adolf told Quinn to come back as he pulled his pistol free and tried to see what was bothering his dog.

Cokey stopped his Oskar-like chatter and pulled his double barrel to his lap.

Adolf said, "No birds are singing. Something is waiting ahead."

Paul yelled out, "What has got into your dog?"

"He senses trouble." Adolf rose in his saddle to look ahead, "Get your gun ready Mr. Adams. Could be an ambush."

"I'm ready. The sight of this big 10 gauge should change anybody's mind."

Adolf didn't think so. Mr. Adams was a great fellow, but was still green about the frontier. "There will be a fight Paul. Could be those Utes or it could be our friends from the fort."

It was the latter. The nine men from the fort rode over the ridge with guns drawn. Adolf's thought was right, Gumbo Pete seemed to be the leader of the outlaws that were robbing and killing.

Adolf didn't give them a chance to fire first. He started firing Mr. Paterson and was happy to hear Cokey's shotgun open fire, sending hot pellets into the bandits. Mr. Adams couldn't risk hitting his two friends, so he jumped off the wagon and ran a few feet away to cut loose with his 10 gauge.

After five shots, Adolf pulled out the cylinder and popped a spare in. Cokey was already letting loose with his own pistol when Adolf started firing again. He sensed pistol shots being fired by Mr. Adams too, but time had slowed for him and he was in a killing zone. He knew that a bullet had tugged his hat from his head and another had ripped through the loose portion of his shirt on his left side. It wasn't until it became quiet that he felt the bullet burn on his shoulder.

Horses were running away, but eight bodies were cluttering the trail. Most were lying still, but two were moaning holding onto whatever life their bodies still clung to. That is when he noticed Gumbo Pete had tried to run away. He hadn't made it. Quinn's mouth was dripping blood and he was standing over the throat-less corpse of Gumbo Pete. Adolf decided that Quinn had gotten a wanted revenge for his two siblings.

"Everyone all right?" Adolf yelled without taking his eyes off the bloody mess ahead.

"Just a burn on the thigh, but I am fine. Probably need to change my drawers," Mr. Adams replied.

Adolf risked a quick glance to the wagon seat beside him when he realized Cokey had not answered. Cokey was still pointing his pistol, but his chest was covered with his blood. "Paul get up here and watch those guys. Cokey has been shot," croaked Adolf.

As soon as Mr. Adams ran forward, Adolf jumped off Buck and climbed onto the wagon. Cokey was still alive, but he had two holes over his left pocket and a third just above his belt on the left side.

"Dang it all to hell. They done killed me, partner."

"I'll stop the bleeding and take you to the post surgeon." Adolf was tearing his shirt into strips when he felt his friend's hand on his arm.

"Adolf, it's no use. I am already cold and the darkness is coming on. I am gone." He looked Adolf in the face, "Oh young Adolf, I am not ready to go. So much more I want to do. It does hurt fierce. Young man, I loves you and want all you's to know that you were good to ride the river with." With that he shivered and fell against Adolf's bare chest.

Adolf hugged his companion and cried out, "It just ain't fair Lord!"

Chapter 44

Today was the big day and a beautiful day it was. The sky was a wonderful azure with cotton tufts of white clouds drifting slowly just above the snowcapped mountain peaks in the west. A gentle breeze was providing motion to the sheets hanging on the clothesline beside the south of the large ranch house, logs squared and aged gray by ten years of harsh rays from the sun.

North of the house stood a huge barn with hay showing through the open door to the loft above two large doors to the entrance. Three mustangs were taking a sip of water from the tank at the bottom of a windmill. The squeaking of the windmill was accented by the sound of Sven's twenty pound hammer shaping a piece of red hot iron laid across his anvil just inside the door of his blacksmith shop.

East of the windmill stood the weathered original bunkhouse. Beside the bunkhouse were split-rail corrals with three quarter horse stallions – a red dun roan, a buckskin, and a frisky black. The black was yelling at the other two to proclaim his right to the choice mares. Another large corral held the saddle horses, including Buck, Blue, Patches, Foxy and Betsy.

The entire valley held over four hundred mustangs in various colors – mares, yearlings, and colts.

Caroline, Neale, and Oskar's pregnant wife, Anna Marie, were catching up on the day's gossip by the flower garden. They kept one eye on the nine kids of various ages scattered over the yard. The two eight-year olds, Sven's oldest boy Olaf, named after his father, and the larger, blond, Sven Jr., were gazing out from the hayloft.

Grouped around the fire pit, daring each other to catch sticks on fire, were Adolf's seven-year old son Paul, named after Caroline's father, Adolf's six-year old Hermann, Sven's large blond seven-year old son Axel, and Oskar's twin six-year old boys Oskar Jr. and Adolf, both with bright red hair and lots of freckles.

The two beautiful five year-old girls, Adolf's Beth and Sven's raven haired Ailish, were sitting at a play table pretending to have a tea party.

The fumes, from the quarter side of buffalo and a half of a pig spitted on barbeques, drifted across the valley. The smell drew insects who were chased by curious red-winged blackbirds and their timid cousins, yellow headed blackbirds.

Today was the day for having a barbeque to celebrate ten years in this valley and Adolf was looking for his best friend Oskar. He was carrying a bottle of vintage brandy and three glasses. He had decided that Oskar and he should join Sven in toasting their anniversary, along with a toast to Cokey's memory, but he couldn't find Oskar.

Then he heard Oskar yelling, "Adolf, come here a minute. I have a question for you." Oskar was standing over Cokey's grave by the quaking aspen grove wearing no hat and a shit-eating grin. Ginger and Rascal were napping by his feet.

Adolf walked towards Oskar with Quinn tagging along. When he got to Oskar he said, "We need to join Sven for a celebration toast." He held up the bottle and glasses."

Oskar said, "First I have a question for you."

Adolf was a little put out that Oskar was not anxious to have their festivity drink, but he stood in front of Oskar and asked, "What do you want to ask?"

Oskar reached out and took ahold of his friend's arm, turning him around to face the valley. He waved his right hand toward their homestead and asked, "What do you see?"

At first Adolf was very puzzled, but as he looked over the valley a vivid flashback memory sprang into his mind. He remembered that morning when he and Oskar stood on this exact spot. It was their first morning in this valley, just before they rode west to see the wild mustangs for the very first time. Ten years ago, he had shared a dream for this valley with Oskar.

Adolf looked back at Oskar and just grinned, ear to ear.

---

[i] Racing Trotters is traced to the Dutch in the 1500's and did not require being wealthy. Later it also become popular in both Europe and the new United States

[ii] Hawken guns were custom made by the Hawken brothers, Jacob and Samuel, for only those who could afford them or were famous, such as Jim Bridger, Kit Carson, and Theodore Roosevelt. The Hawken brothers were located in St. Louis,

Missouri and their rifles became referred to as the "plains rifle" or the "Rocky Mountain Rifles" when the fur trade opened up in the mountains.

[iii] The combination of the Treaty of Chicago of 1821 and the Treaty of Mississinwas of 1826 had succeeded in transplanting tribes into the more western territories, but isolated splinter groups for many tribes refused to leave. All government treaties were rescinded later when settlers wanted the land.

[iv] The Kanzas tribe lived in central Kansas and stealing horses was just part of their way of life. They didn't steal to trade or eat, but a form of obtaining power. It was common for one brave to have more than one hundred horses. He could improve his status by giving them to chiefs to get special treatment or to a prospective father-in-law to impress with his prowess. The Kansas Territory was named after them.

[v] The Colt Paterson was young Samuel Colt's first step into the making of revolvers. With the assistance of John Paterson they created the five shot revolver with a folding hidden trigger and no trigger guard. The cocking of the hammer engaged the trigger.

[vi] The Fox Trotters was developed from gaited horses in Tennessee, Kentucky, and Virginia. Breeds that were used included Arabian, Morgan, American Saddlebred, Tennessee Walking Horse and Standardbred. By the time Missouri became a state in 1821 the Missouri Fox Trotters were already known for their unique gait.

[vii] In 1822, William Becknell had led the first trading party over the Santa Fe Trail and returned with a herd of Mexican mules and donkeys. Industrious men recognized that these hardy animals were going to be a necessity for pulling the wagons of future settlers the rough miles traveling west. They started the breeding of Missouri Mules.

[viii] The vast Delaware tribe was referred to by other tribes as Lenape, signifying original man. Their claim of superiority was recognized by other tribes who also accorded them the title of 'Grandfather'. Theirs was the first treaty made by the United States in 1778 at Fort Pitt and it was contemplated by the sixth article that

the intent was the possible formation of an Indian State headed by the Delaware. Of course, the treaty was broken later by the government.

[ix] The Shawnee used the name *Chelolah* and other tribes called it the *Okesee-sebo*. When John McCoy surveyed the area, he referred to it as the Smoky Hill similar to Fremont's name *Smoky Hills Fork*. Rumor is that a common great bend landmark of isolated buttes looked like hazy smoke from a distance.

[x] The log fort was built for fur trappers in 1834 on the Laramie's fork. Although built by the Sublette and Campbell trading company, Fontenelle, Fitzpatrick & Company purchased it in 1835. They resold it in 1936 to Pierre Chouteau and The American Fur Company with their trapping brigade known as the Rocky Mountain Outfit. The logs had become dilapidated by 1941 and the competition of Lancaster Lupton's Fort Platte required the old fort to be torn down and a new adobe fort built at a cost of $10,000. The replacement fort had been named Fort John.